The Vanishing Bloodstain

Greed, resentment, and murder

BOOK TWO

AGNES MAKÓCZY

For information contact :
www.agnes-makoczy.com

Book Cover Image
Josh Applegate @joshapplegate
Photo by Josh Applegate on Unsplash

Book formatting by Derek Murphy from www.CreativIndie.com

ISBN: 9780977439591
First Edition: July 2016

Contents

Introduction

Roderick Bingham and the Lost Gold

RODERICK BINGHAM KNEW what kind of lowly, worthless bastard he was. He also knew he was a determined and relentless sort of bastard. He rode the carriage to the clearing in the woods, told his horses to be quiet and walked the rest of the way, picking his steps carefully in the dark.

"There you are," Elsa whispered from behind the tree trunk by the outhouse. "I thought you had changed your mind."

"Dear Elsa, you're the love of my life. I would never…"

"Yes, yes, I know, but we must hurry up. It's almost time for the household to wake up."

"Do you have everything?"

"Of course. By the back gate. Maisy helped me bring it down."

"All right, then. I'll fetch one of the horses. I'll meet you there."

"Do hurry up."

Roderick Bingham hurried with his horse to the back gate, doing his best to blend in with the morning mist. The air was chilly, and steam was pouring from the nostrils of the restless horse. Roderick was restless as well, but for a completely different reason. What if it was a mistake to run away with Elsa? What if they were pursued and captured? If Sir John was compassionate, Elsa might be forgiven. But what about him? Surely he would be hanged.

Elsa and her maid were waiting for him and helped load the gold on the back of the horse. Terrified, Maisy disappeared as soon as she was allowed. And then, Elsa faced Roderick and looked into his eyes, trying to look into his soul.

"You won't leave me behind, will you?"

"Of course not. I might be a swindler and a crook, but I'm madly in love with you, and I would go to the dark pits of hell itself for you. You know that."

"Because you know what will happen if John finds out, don't you?"

"Please, fear not. You're coming with me one way, or the other. And we'll have a wonderful life together. Forever."

Elsa hung on to Roderick as long as she dared, treasuring the warmth of his breath on her shoulder, and the heartbeats under his shirt. Why was she so afraid? By and by, she had to let go. Roderick gave her one last long kiss, and looked into her clear blue eyes. "I will love you forever," he said, and then walked away quietly into the forest with his horse restlessly snorting behind him. Elsa did love her Roderick dearly, but had this horrible foreboding in her heart.

Meantime, Roderick was very pleased with himself. The first part of the plan had worked to perfection. There was enough gold in his carriage to keep him and Elsa in luxury for the rest of their lives. Now, less than two hours later, it was almost dawn, and he was headed for the creek to perform the second part of his plan.

Down by the creek, the mist rose from around the unspoiled gurgling water, and it spilled out of the forests that loomed dark behind it. The air was cold and crisp, and it smelled of the illegal fires that the poor and the homeless roasted their poached ducks and pigs on, safe in the darkness from the cruel eyes of the local Sheriff.

Roderick Bingham looked around. He was the first one at the clearing. He heard the crunching of footsteps behind his back almost immediately, and turned around, pistol at the ready.

"Oh, it's you, Freddy. I thought I was the first one here."

"Good morning to you too, cousin. I saw you step out of the fog, and had the sudden feeling that this is a very bad idea. You still have time to change your mind. You could misfire, thereby satisfying your honor. It's not like you'll get hurt. Everyone knows what a bad shot Sir John is."

"No, Freddy. There's no other way out. I have to do this. Go home if you don't want to be here. I'll be okay."

"I wish I could believe that. Are those horses I hear?"

"Yes. They're coming. Wish me luck."

Roderick and Freddy looked toward the sound, and saw two beautiful horses and two tall, elegant, well dressed men riding them into the clearing. Roderick heard in his imagination the drums of the executioner, and he gulped. This was it, then.

Sir John and his Second dismounted, and approached Roderick and the unhappy cousin. They greeted each other coldly, but politely.

Looking at Sir John, Roderick couldn't help but compare himself to the older and more honorable man, and he felt like a worm. He had caused this situation by his reckless behavior, all to satisfy his urge to seduce another man's wife. He was no better than a worm, and for a second, he wished himself to be somewhere else, and not in this absurd pretense of chivalry. Shouldn't he escape now? He could make a run for it. He had the gold. The carriage was loaded, and he had his ship ticket. All he had to do was get to Dover by night-time, unseen. Once he made it across the Channel into France, he would be untouchable.

No. Better to kill Sir John. There would be no one left to remember the missing gold. Elsa would meet him at the docks, and they would sail into their future—together forever—for whatever it was worth. But, for that, he had to kill Sir John.

The sun was finally coming up, illuminating the little patch of clearing where he was going to kill a man to abscond with his wife and his gold. They stood back to back, him and Sir John. With loaded pistols in hand, they walked ten paces as they had agreed. Roderick knew he was an excellent shot. He could kill a rat at twenty paces. A man at ten would be nothing. Then, they turned around and faced each other.

The Second gave the signal and dropped the handkerchief. The two men started walking toward each other, pistols at the ready. The sun, coming up finally—behind Roderick's back—illuminated into the eyes of Sir John, blinding him, and Roderick again hated himself for having chosen the best spot on purpose. Sir John had so little experience in duels. On the other hand, how many men had he, Roderick killed? He had lost count a long time ago. But this kill was different. He cursed Elsa. Something about her had changed him. He didn't want to kill anymore.

In slow motion, the handkerchief started billowing in the gentle breeze as it fell, and Roderick pressed his finger on the trigger. He saw his opponent's fat little bullet leave the barrel one second after his did. And then he saw—to his horror—Elsa running across the clearing, screaming.

"Stop, please stop," she was yelling. "Please don't shoot!" He remembered turning toward her, and making signs for her to stay away because the bullets had been fired, but it all happened in an instant, and she didn't see him. She ran blindly into the path of the bullets, not thinking, her arms flailing, trying to stop what had already happened.

Roderick knew it before he saw it. Elsa's legs buckled under her, and an ugly stain started spreading on her pretty yellow morning dress. Her eyes seemed to be looking at the sun: big, surprised, and baffled. Then, she was dead on the ground. Behind her, her husband, a gaping wound on his chest—walking still—God only knew with what unearthly strength, howled in anger at the death of his wife. But Sir John was a dead man walking, and he had no more bullets in his pistol.

THE VANISHING BLOODSTAIN

Roderick, knowing that he was safe, jumped on his horse to get away. Meantime, back at the clearing, his cousin and Sir John's Second stared in disbelief at the spectacle of horror in front of them. And Roderick, knowing that he had caused the death of the woman he loved, jumped on his horse and vanished into history.

Chapter 1

Father Armand Visits An Old Friend

FATHER ARMAND WAS AGING WELL. Tall, slender, dark wavy hair, with the slightly eccentric look of a stage magician, you had to admit that he looked good for a middle-aged priest. Trying hard to ignore the sin of vanity, Father Armand took long, manly steps toward St. John's Cathedral in Lafayette—his old parish—enjoying the way that his *soutane* billowed elegantly against his ankles. Father Armand looked up at the familiar bell tower rising clearly toward a clean blue sky. A few birds, a few lingering clouds, that was all. Just as ephemeral as human life itself.

Marcel was dying. Marcel had been his best friend through the years of college, and then seminary, since the days when—with stars in their eyes—they still believed they could make a difference in an increasingly evil world. They had traveled to South America together, spreading the Good Word among the tribes in the Andes Mountains and the jungles of the Amazon River Basin. Now, his dear friend was dying, and Father Armand, who had consoled so many kinds of grieves and sorrows in his lifetime, had no idea what he was going to tell his friend.

It was a lovely Louisiana spring day: high pressure, barely a cloud in the deep blue sky. If anything, it was a good day to die. Back in the yard, among the multicolored spring flowers, behind the lovely old church, someone had kindly arranged for Marcel to sit in the sun, perhaps for the last time ever, and enjoy the chaos of nature that he was about to leave behind. The nurse brought Father Armand a chair, and he sat companionably with Marcel, holding his emaciated hand, reminiscing about youth and good times and speculating on the kingdom of heaven. Then, Marcel closed his eyes—as if he had gotten tired of all the sun—and quietly stopped breathing. It had been a good day to die.

With a heavy heart, Father Armand turned the car toward Old Plantation Road. Now he wished he hadn't promised Carolyn to go visit her, but he couldn't take his promise back. Carolyn was old, and had a leg in the grave. He couldn't begrudge her this small token of affection, for old times' sake. Who knew if he would ever see her again?

Old Plantation Road is an anomaly in an otherwise rather large and bustling town. Hidden behind a thicket of impassable poison ivy bushes and wild blackberry thorns, it's an invisible sanctuary of enormous, centenarian live oak trees growing alongside a one-way dirt road that's just about impossible to see from the busy street. People have lived and died all their lives in Lafayette, without ever knowing that such a rare hidden place exists. Only two plantation homes remain, built on plenty of land, quite a bit back from the dead-end road.

Father Armand parked at the end of the dirt road by the azalea bushes, and walked back toward the house. The silence was absolute, except for the occasional crunching of pebbles under his feet. He took his time. He treasured the few moments of absolute solace, and the stillness around him. Back here, on this lonesome dirt road, the passage of time had no meaning. Back here, there was no one else but you, and God, and the universe.

The rambling old plantation home had seen better days. Once upon a time probably full of owners, slaves, and servants, now it seemed empty and forgotten. Fallen limbs from the last storm hadn't been picked up. There were greenish mildew growths on the peeling columns, and the Virginia creeper ivy, that had once been planted with such care—he remembered—had now overtaken every empty spot around the house, threatening to strangle the stately old trees, and pretty soon the house itself as well. Carolyn probably didn't care about worldly things like mildew and fallen tree limbs anymore.

He rang the doorbell and waited for quite a long time. Memories of things forgotten came rushing back as if they had happened yesterday. He remembered Carolyn returning to Louisiana with her brand new British husband. Back then, her family plantation home had stood empty for decades, and had been allowed to decay to a crumbling hulk, and Carolyn's rich British husband had spent a fortune restoring it. They even had an enormous sun-room built completely out of glass out back. But even if the sun-room was still there after all those years, he doubted any sunshine would manage to squeeze through the overgrown tree canopy that now protected the house.

The majestic carved door was opened by a butler in old-fashioned livery. Small, frail looking, with big inquisitive eyes, he shuffled in front of Father Armand solemnly—taking his time—as he led him through the labyrinthine dusty house full of generations' worth of art collections, and heavy, uncomfortable looking furniture, to the large, bright and colorful sun-room in the back, where Carolyn sat, expecting him.

Father Armand took one look at his friend and former parishioner, and burst out laughing. He had expected to find a shriveled old woman with a wrinkled sour face, with a leg in the grave. Instead, he saw very much the old Carolyn he remembered, pretty, plump, funny, and with a sparkling good disposition. She was dressed in a flattering flowery dress, wearing too much jewelry, and sat on an exotic looking chair, propped up by large, colorful pillows. He gave her a big hug, grateful that she was so alive.

THE VANISHING BLOODSTAIN

"How wonderful to see you, Armand. It's been a long time. You look so good," she told him with a big happy laugh, pinching his cheeks gently. Of all the people in the world, Carolyn was the only person allowed such disrespect toward his eminent self. He loved it.

"You're the one who looks amazing."

"You thought I was shriveled up and dying, didn't you?" She laughed with a twinkle in her eyes. "Well, I have no intention of dying yet. As a matter of fact, I'm delighted that you're here, Armand, because today is my 80th birthday and you can help me celebrate it."

At that moment, the butler slowly shuffled into the sun-room, solemnly pushing a tea tray on wheels, laden with a heavy silver tea set, and an endless display of cheeses, sandwiches, fruits and other delights. Father Armand suddenly remembered how hungry he was, and jumped up to help.

"No, no, Armand, don't get up. It's good for him to feel needed, to help him stay young." Carolyn turned toward him and winked, but Father Armand had his doubts. Regardless, he sat impatiently while the elderly butler shuffled on toward them at an excruciatingly slow pace, pushing the cart with shaking hands that made the silver rattle.

A middle-aged exotic woman in foreign looking clothes stepped into the room, and took over. She served tea efficiently, and said very little, all of it with a slightly foreign accent that Father Armand had no idea what to do with. But he did service to the food. Suddenly, he was famished, and grateful, and excited to be alive, all at the same time. The sandwiches were excellent.

"So, who else is coming to your party?" he asked Carolyn between mouthfuls of spicy chicken sandwich. "Anyone I know?"

"Well, there are the neighbors. You might remember them: the Lanes. Sanders and Laura Lane."

"Sanders Lane, the senator, and his wife? Yes. I remember the Lanes. They were fond of playing tennis and drinking margaritas, weren't they?" Father Armand licked his fingers discreetly and reached for another spicy chicken sandwich.

"Yes, them. They still are. Fond of drinking margaritas, that is. The Shady Lanes, we used to call them. They live in the only other big house on this road. They haven't been to church much since you left Lafayette. I bet they used to have a lot to confess," Carolyn told him with a grin.

"Now Carolyn, don't be nosy. You know I can't tell." But they both laughed lightly.

"Then there are my three friends from college: Dolly, Dotty and Renée. They're in a nursing home out in Youngsville. It's a lovely place, flowers everywhere. Renée's chauffer is bringing them. I can't believe I've known them for almost 60 years."

"I can't believe they're still alive. I remember them well. You four were in charge of the flowers and the gossip at the Cathedral."

"Well, we still gossip too much. And now that they've gotten older, Dolly and Dotty look like twins. They always looked alike, didn't they? They're still pretty spunky, but Renée needs a walker to get around. Then let's see. Oh, yes, I almost forgot to tell you. I met the long-lost daughter of my little sister. She appeared one day on the front steps. Knocked on the door. She has just arrived from India with her husband. He's a very nice young man, the quiet type. She, I don't know. I'll have to work hard at becoming fond of her. There is something about her that makes me very uncomfortable. But him, I like very much."

"I've never heard you mention a niece."

"I know. I was quite surprised myself that she decided to come live here. We're not close. My parents had my sister very late in life. I was about to come back to the United States for college when Mother found out she was expecting. After that, I only saw them sporadically, because India was so far away. My little sister isn't very friendly. She married some Indian aristocrat there. So there you go. My niece probably takes after her.

"Then, there's my grandson. Well, John's grandson, Claude. He's such a dear boy. He's so busy, but he always has time for his grand-mère. He's engaged, and so he's bringing his fiancée today. I haven't met her yet.

"My attorney and his wife are also coming. You might remember them: Alfred and Lila Bailey. She's a lovely creature. Rich, beautiful, much younger than her husband. She could have married anyone, and yet she picked Alfred. The heart wants what the heart wants, you know. Anyway, they've always been very thick with the Lanes. They play tennis together."

"I do remember them. Alfred was involved in some kind of scandal years back with an overseas company, but he was cleared, wasn't he? I never met Lila."

"You'll like her. She's a personable and classy young woman. Last but not least, Dr. Schroeder is coming as well, with his wife."

"I thought you weren't on speaking terms with Desmond after the medication mix-up that killed your husband."

"I wasn't for many years. But I know it wasn't his fault. It was the hospital. Poor John. He was very fond of Desmond. I couldn't let a good friendship be ruined by blaming him for something he didn't do."

"That was very Christian of you."

Father Armand sat back on the rattan chair, and allowed his body to sink pleasantly into the feathery pillows, while Carolyn chatted on. He sipped on his tea. It tasted of foreign lands, and coconut trees, and golden sands reaching into a deep blue sea. He was happy he had bothered to come visit after all.

Chapter 2

Parvati

PARVATI WAS ANNOYED. She was tired of visiting the old aunt, and tired of having to kiss up to her. So she was taking it out on her husband. On second thought, she was tired of her spineless husband Matt as well. She wished they'd stayed in India, even with all the heat and the overpopulation. It was better than Lafayette, where everyone had beautiful homes, and cars, and pretty things, and she didn't have the money for any of that. With their luck, Carolyn was going to live forever, and they'd be old before she got her inheritance.

"Do you have to drive so slowly?" she asked him with impatience. "We're going to be the last ones there. For once, I would like to arrive on time, before that whiny Claude gets all the attention."

"Nothing wrong with arriving a little late, darling," he told her, trying to appease her. "Besides, I can't go any faster in this rickety old thing."

"We would be there already if you'd taken the feeder road instead. Now we're stuck in this stupid traffic." Parvati looked out the window at the mile-long line of cars at the red light ahead of them. How many more red lights would come and go before they got through?

"We're stuck in this stupid traffic because I don't know my way around. I keep telling you to help me with the map, but what do you do? Just whine, whine, and pick on me."

"You know I don't know how to read a map. If the old cow had given us a better car, we would have a GPS in it like all the decent people."

"It won't be long now," Matt told her, and reached out to pat her leg. "Quit worrying so much. Soon, we'll have all the money in the world, and we'll get us the fanciest car they have for sale."

"But only if we can get rid of Claude. Or else, she'll leave him everything." Matt looked at his wife. She was pouting unhappily, with her arms crossed over her chest.

"True," he said. "But it won't be easy."

Chapter 3

The Guests Arrive

WITH AN AIR OF DIGNITY, the diminutive butler announced Dr. Schroeder and Madame Schroeder. Father Armand turned toward the doorway and saw a tired looking older man following his wife into the room. He wore an awkward comb-over over his shiny bald pate, and the once well-tailored clothes now hung on him like they belonged to a much bigger, much prouder man.

Dr. Schroeder hadn't been young in a very long time, but his wife was. And she looked like an expensive woman, too. Not that Father Armand knew for sure, and he didn't want to be uncharitable in his thinking, but it seemed to him that her clothes were extremely expensive, and her numerous jewels real. Just look at the size of that diamond ring.

Dr. Schroeder looked tired. Desmond Schroeder had been a tall and arrogant man once, but he had aged tremendously in the years since Father Armand had last seen him, and now he walked stooped over. He followed his wife to the sun-room obediently, and after amenities were exchanged, he sat down by her mechanically, as if he wasn't much interested in being there. Father Armand, a *connoisseur* of human nature, guessed that keeping up with his much younger wife was what had the good doctor looking so haggard.

Suddenly, ending the tedium, three cheerful voices barged into the sun-room, singing a Happy Birthday a Capella. Carolyn jumped up and went to greet her friends, and Father Armand instantly forgot how bored he had been just seconds ago.

Dolly and Dotty were delightful. They really looked like two peas in a pod. Small and plump, with purplish white permed hair and matching reading glasses hanging from chains around their necks, they gesticulated with their walking canes in hand, risking poking someone's eyes out, laughing, and hugging, and exchanging amenities. Renée, shriveled, and no longer plump, was quieter. Her skin was sallow, and there were big black circles under her eyes. But she looked happy to be there. The three old women behaved like prisoners on their day out, and maybe that's what living in a nursing home was like. Father Armand shuddered, and vowed to himself never to live that long.

After some fuss, Dolly, Dotty, and Renée, finally settled down on a rattan sofa, side by side—like birds on a perch—and the foreign maid arranged some pillows around them for comfort. Gossip was flying high as the friends sampled the sandwiches and cakes that the maid had placed on their laps.

"Is that new?" Dolly and Dotty asked, almost in unison, when they noticed the gold bracelet heavily inset with pieces of green stone that looked like emeralds, on Carolyn's wrist. "Can we hold it?" one of them asked.

"Sure, here you go," she told them, and handed the extravagant trinket to the old girls. Father Armand watched the women fondle the bracelet greedily, surprised at the glint of envy in their eyes. "I bought it as a birthday present to myself," Carolyn said with a big happy smile.

"Are the stones real?" Dolly asked. She reached out for the bracelet with avarice, and quickly snatched it out of Dotty's hands. "I could kill for something this beautiful."

"Yes, of course they're real. They're authentic emeralds too, not crystals. So hard to find these days," Carolyn told her friend cheerfully.

"You should get yourself one too, Dolly. They had them with rubies, and garnets, and other stones."

Father Armand was amazed that after 60 years, these four still hadn't run out of things to talk about. They behaved like high school kids. For a short while, the underlying envy in Dolly's and Dotty's voice made him squirm, but soon the conversation veered toward the famous new niece, and Carolyn broke into an extended version of how the young woman's visit had come about. Meantime, Renée kept looking at the doctor with her wrinkled eyebrows scrunched.

"You look familiar," she finally told him, pushing her glasses up her nose bridge. "You remind me of a boy I used to know. Jimmy or Johnny, I think he was called. We went to the same school, took some classes together. He was going to become a chemist, or something, but he was having a hard time keeping up. Funny things, memories, how they come and go. Some days I can remember my life so clearly, but others, I almost forget my own name. Anyway, that was a long time ago. He must have dropped out of school because I never saw him again." Renée shook her head, and then turned back to her friends and continued chatting. Dr. Schroeder and his wife looked at each other, and the doctor shrugged.

The tea was flowing. Father Armand—who never drank the stuff himself—was surprised by how much he was enjoying it. Refreshing and aromatic, it smoothed down all the delicious hors d'oeuvres the maid kept bringing out from the kitchen. This was turning out to be a soothing ending for a sad day. The drive from Lafayette had been long and tedious, and he suddenly realized how tired he was. With the humdrum of the conversation providing background noise around him, he quietly leaned his head against the back of the tall armchair, and dozed off.

He was awakened by excited voices coming from the front door. A bossy young woman in startlingly bright clothes and jangling jewelry, and a shy young man with glasses, stepped into the room, and brought everyone back to life.

"Happy Birthday, Auntie," the woman said in a loud, unflattering sing-song voice, and hustled over to where Carolyn was sitting, and put in her arms an enormous bunch of flowers and a box covered in gift-wrap. "Hello, everyone. I'm Parvati, and this is my husband Matt." The young woman looked around and smiled a little tight smile at everyone, and settled down next to her aunt with an inelegant plop.

"Well, it's nice to be here before Claude, for once," Parvati told no one in particular. "He always gets all the attention. Sometimes, I even think that you love him more than you love me." Parvati's unfriendly face was smirking. "Even though I am your real family."

"Of course she loves me more," a deep, pleasant voice exclaimed from the hallway as the beloved grandson stepped into the room. "I've been here for her all along, whereas you showed up like, what, a couple of weeks ago? Hello, everyone, we are Claude and Valeria, newly engaged. Happy Birthday, grand-mère. You look gorgeous today. Here's a present for you." He bent down to kiss Carolyn, and whispered in her ear, "I picked it out all by myself. I hope you like it." Father Armand, who was close enough to hear, smiled.

There was much excitement among the aging crowd at the arrival of the young people, with their loud stories and their enthusiasm. Dolly, Dotty and Renée listened with rapt attention at the young folks, who were trying to outdo each other with their stories, competing for everyone's attention. Parvati had just started on one about Dona Paula Beach on the island of Goa, where the daughter of a Portuguese Viceroy had jumped off a cliff, and now haunted the place, when two middle-aged couples followed the butler to the room.

"We're so sorry to be late," someone said apologetically, and all four approached the birthday girl for hugs and presents. One of them put two large bottles of champagne into the maid's hands, and someone handed her another enormous bouquet of flowers. They were a sleek bunch these four, Father Armand noticed. It had been a long time, but he remembered them very well. They still looked ambitious and hungry. Hungry for power and money. Nothing had changed.

"It's time you arrived, you four. I'm famished," Carolyn told them, wagging a finger at them with mock disapproval, all the while smiling at them. "Everyone, these are Alfred—my attorney—and his lovely wife Lila, and these are my neighbors, Sanders and Laura Lane. Now say a quick hello everyone, and let's go eat."

Dinner was announced, and the guests happily jostled each other to the dining room, following the spicy aromas of Cajun food. "What's on the menu tonight, grand-mère?" Claude asked his grandmother.

Carolyn was leaning on Claude's arm as they walked to the dining room, and Father Armand was walking right behind them.

"All your favorites," he heard her say. "Corn and crab bisque first, and then crawfish étouffée, with sweet potato pecan pie for dessert. But just for you, dear boy, the cook made some Carencro Kicking Shrimp, knowing how much you like it. For being so kind to your old grand-mère."

Father Armand slowly followed Carolyn and her grandson, salivating at the menu. When he looked up, he noticed the twinkle in young Claude's eyes as he looked at his grandmother, and the affection with which Carolyn looked back at him. It made him feel good that she had someone in her life that loved her, and cared enough for her to come visit her. And yet, he couldn't shake off the impression that there was among all these nice people an undercurrent of malice in all their friendliness, but alas he couldn't pinpoint where it was coming from.

Chapter 4

Dinner

SITTING DOWN AROUND THE ENORMOUS dining room table was a noisy affair. Suddenly, everyone was in a talkative mood, pulling and pushing chairs, arguing about the seating. Father Armand was shown to the head of the table, and he protested, but was voted down. Carolyn—the birthday girl—sat opposite him. Her three college friends, the attorney and his wife, and the neighbors, sat to her right. The young people, and the doctor and his wife, sat to her left.

There was an awkward moment when Father Armand was asked to say a blessing, but nobody would stop talking. He shrugged and smiled, and said it by himself, quietly. Wine was flowing, and memorable events were being remembered between spoonfuls of corn and crab bisque. People were laughing, and chatting, and enjoying each other's company. As usual—when he was having a good time at a family gathering—Father Armand felt a brief moment of regret at not having a family of his own. Christmases, Thanksgivings, and birthdays, were always spent alone, unless someone remembered to invite him. But it passed swiftly. It usually did.

With the arrival of the sweet potato and pecan pie, people sat back comfortably in their chairs to sip on their wine, and the conversation finally turned to the well-known family mystery of the bloodstain on the rug. It was the type of story that families were fond of rehashing every time there was a get-together. It was a terrible story. A young man had died in the foyer many years earlier, and had bled out on the big blue rug. The bloodstain had been impossible to remove completely, and because the house had remained empty for such a long time, it had eventually dried, and faded, and blended, into the design of the rug. Father Armand drank his wine down, and served himself another wedge of pie.

"Well, one morning I woke up, and the bloodstain was gone. I couldn't believe my eyes. It is really gone," Carolyn said triumphantly. Everyone looked at her disappointed. Obviously, it had been a treasured family story that would be no more. "Go see for yourselves, if you don't believe me." Carolyn looked toward the door where the maid had appeared with a fresh bowl of whipped cream, and smiled at her. "Sharmila says she washed it out. Quite amazing, isn't she? I hope it doesn't appear again."

"Maybe it's like the Canterbury Ghost, and the bloodstain will continue appearing until the murder is solved," Valeria said, surprising everyone by saying something.

"It's not the Canterbury Ghost, my dear," corrected Claude with a superior voice. "It's the Canterville Ghost, and the story has nothing to do with murder."

"Oh, whatever. Someone should try to solve the murder anyway."

This started another loud discussion about bloodstains and dead bodies, and then Renée looked at the guests sitting across from her, and began rambling.

"Now I remember. There was a party in this house. It was many, many years ago. We were all here." Renée's voice had become dull and hypnotic. Everyone went silent, listening to her every word. Her eyes had lost focus. She was lost in her memories.

"We were all dancing and drinking, and the music was so loud. And then something happened, and there was a fight. It was Johnny Lagasse arguing with someone. He was drunk. They were both drunk.

THE VANISHING BLOODSTAIN

And next thing he was dead. There was blood everywhere. I remember all the blood. They said it was an accident. But it wasn't. His face was all beaten up so badly, they couldn't recognize him. It was horrible. He bled out on that rug." Renée's vacuous eyes looked far into the past. Her head was turned downward and to her right, as if she was staring at the beaten up dead body of the young man. "I remember it all so clearly. That's why the bloodstain has been on it all this time. It's very hard to get a bloodstain out."

The guests were all horrified. This was too much information. They sighed with relief when the maid brought out the cake and the champagne, and someone said "speech" and Carolyn got up. She looked at everyone at the table and smiled. For one brief second, she looked like the cat that had just swallowed the canary—mighty pleased with herself, and Father Armand shivered with foreboding. Then she began talking, and her speech knocked everyone's socks off.

"Dear friends and family, let's not talk about sad things. Not today. Thank you all for coming to celebrate my birthday with me. Before we cut the cake, I wanted to tell you all that—as some of you may already know—I've decided to make some changes to my will. Alfred has been trying to talk me out of it, but it's been decided. And I'm going to hide the will somewhere in this house. That way you'll get to look for it, like a treasure hunt. Just for fun. I thought you'd all get a kick out of that. But don't get too excited. I'm not planning on dying any time soon. I still have a few years left in me. And don't ask me who's getting what, because I won't tell. I want it to be a surprise. Now where's that champagne? Let's toast."

Father Armand watched the astonished guests surrounding Carolyn go absolutely silent, dumbstruck, as if a bomb had gone off in their midst. Most of the guests had already gotten up from their chairs and were milling around Carolyn, waiting for champagne and birthday hugs, when she broke the news.

Agnes Makóczy

Father Armand, who had remained seated to give the family their space, watched as everyone's eyes and mouths popped open in shock. He could almost see the wheels of greed turning in their brains, wondering if they were about to be cut from the new will altogether, and for a second or two, everyone was completely still, caught in a tableau of overwhelming confusion. Then, they began talking again nervously, all at once, and way too loud, pretending to be cheerful, but Father Armand could tell that the party spirit was gone. Someone asked if the will was legal if it was hidden like that, and Alfred Bailey said yes, of course. It was signed and official.

Then, the champagne was passed around soberly, and everyone toasted the birthday girl with forced enthusiasm. It was drunk in big disappointed gulps for moral fortitude, and Father Armand figured nobody had really tasted it. Carolyn, oblivious to the mess she had created around her, smiled cheerfully at her loved ones and took a sip of the champagne, but her big brown mutt—called Mutt—picked that precise moment to dash into the dining room, and onto Carolyn's lap. In the commotion, she had barely managed to taste her champagne, and then it was all spilled on the floor.

Dolly, Dotty, and Renée, screamed. Someone ran to the kitchen to get the maid. The butler shuffled into the room apologizing to all. He had been taking the dog for a quick walk when he got overexcited by the sound of people in the sun-room, and ran away from him. Mutt looked up happily at the guests with his tongue lolling, and his tail wagging, and then quickly lapped up the champagne on the floor before he was led outside. By the time everyone calmed down and looked around, Carolyn was a heap on the floor, lying there as if dead, with her hand around her throat.

Among the guests, four pairs of eyes looked away from the heap on the floor, and looked at each other. Except for one of them, they all had the faintest smile of anticipation shining in them. They all quickly looked away again, and pretended to be shocked. But horrified, Father Armand had seen it all.

Chapter 5

Father Armand Asks For Help

FATHER ARMAND SAT IN MARGO FONTAINE'S opulent living room, waiting impatiently. Two well-nourished cats watched him curiously from an armchair where they were sprawled together, keeping him company. He arranged the soutane around his ankles with deliberate movements. He was not a man used to asking for favors. He studied first his shoes, and then his nails, unnecessarily. Ever since their last case together, he and Margo Fontaine had put their acrimony to the side and called for truce. It was turning out that they rather liked each other, and enjoyed each other's company. But regardless, a big favor was still a big favor.

It had been a while since his last visit to the rambling old Half Moon Bay home that Margo had moved back into a couple of years earlier. He looked around and saw, to his joy, that the stately home was slowly being renovated. Father Armand loved historic buildings and his heart always twisted with regret when a beautiful old house was torn down to build a modern monstrosity in its place.

Margo's family had built the sea-side house over two hundred years earlier. Even thought it continued to be lived in—on and off—it had become neglected after a series of storms that regularly swept through the bay. This house had once been their crowning glory. Extremely rich as they had been, they were collectors of arts and beautiful things. They travelled the world buying up everything that pleased them and that would add beauty and comfort to their family home. Before Margo took over the restoration project, the lovely mansion had been in serious danger of collapsing. Much of what had made it so alluring and splendid had rotted away or been eaten up by the mildew. Even now, the work was ongoing, and there was still much left to do.

As Father Armand sipped on the aromatic black tea that Lucy—Margo's housekeeper—had served, he wondered what had happened to his universe that he had become a tea-drinking man. Miniature key-lime pies and cucumber sandwiches that appeared with the tea tested his resolve of moderation. In the end, he talked himself into tasting one, just one, and reached out for a bite-sized pie. Louisiana was a food lover's paradise.

Finally, he saw Margo approach from the library. There was always an air of sadness about her, even when she smiled. She would never be tall, nor would she ever be too slender, but the mousey and insecure girl that he once knew had transformed into a pretty young brunette who was kind, determined, and very efficient. Apart from being a choir member at his church of St. Quintian, Margo was now a full-fledged Private Detective, still learning the ropes, but one who took great pride in her ability to solve mysteries and murders. And from what Father Armand had heard, she was very good at it too.

When she approached, he stood up, and she gave him a big hug. Father Armand never knew what to do with a hug, and he squirmed ever so slightly. She was way too familiar with him, and that made him mildly uncomfortable.

"I'm sorry for keeping you waiting, Father Armand," she told him with a big friendly grin. "I had to take that phone call." Margo sat down opposite him, and the cats immediately jumped down from their chair, and with one smooth and elegant move, onto her lap. She stroked their fur lovingly, and they mewled sweetly in appreciation.

"Are those Jenny's cats?" the priest asked, remembering having heard the story of Margo taking them in after her friend's death.

"Yes, they are. Aren't they beautiful? They needed a home, and I couldn't bear the thought of them ending up in a shelter, or worse, being put to death after a few weeks in a cage because nobody had adopted them. They're my babies now. They comfort me."

In between sips of tea, Father Armand told Margo about his visit to Lafayette.

"Carolyn was having a wonderful time." Father Armand arranged the hem of his soutane again with elegant, slender fingers as he tried to remember details. "She lifted her champagne flute. I was watching her. She took a sip." He nodded to himself. His eyes were focused on the distant events. "Then, there was a commotion because of the dog, and the butler came in and took it away, and next thing I knew, she was sprawled on the floor clutching her neck." Father Armand looked at Margo, who was scribbling in a little black leather notebook. "Immediately, the old doctor was all business. He told someone to call an ambulance and kneeled down by her and checked her pulse. Then he said "everyone needs to leave now," and we were all shown to the door by the servants and sent on our way."

"And someone called an ambulance."

"Yes. I heard the call being made. Margo, I'm sure someone tried to poison her." He insisted. "Her hand was on her throat as if she was unable to breathe."

"Tell me again, Father Armand, who brought out the champagne?"

"It was the foreign maid, I think. The champagne flutes were already on the sidebar on trays."

"So the maid opened the bottles in the dining room? Two bottles, right?"

"Yes. Two. I remember two big pops. But I can't tell you who opened them. The guests were milling around Carolyn, to congratulate her."

"And someone poured the champagne," prompted Margo.

"Yes, but I don't remember who. Sorry. I'm afraid I'm not very observant. I guess if I had known something bad was about to happen, I would have paid more attention. Wait," he suddenly said out loud, sitting up straight, and his index finger went up in the air. "I just remembered something."

"What's that?" Margo asked, excited all of a sudden.

"There was someone else in the room. Someone who didn't belong."

"Man, woman?"

"Just a shadow in the doorway. I have to think about it. I'll let you know if I remember anything."

"That's good. Now, you mentioned, Father, that Carolyn didn't like everyone in the room. Do you remember?"

"Yes. She doesn't like her niece. She's loud and opinionated, and she wears bracelets that jingle when she moves. They're very annoying. They grate the nerves. I got the impression that she's not too fond of her neighbors either. I remember that Sanders used to be the conceited type. He was a senator for a long time. But now, he's just cloying. Needy, always trying to be close to Carolyn, to sit next to her. I think it irritates her. She seems to like Lila, the attorney's wife, but maybe not the husband so much. I've known Alfred a long time. He's not as straight an arrow as some people would like to think."

"All right. Let's get back to the others. Who knew about the changes to the will?"

"Oh, I don't know for sure. Obviously, Alfred Bailey. He's her attorney. And maybe Alfred told his wife. She loves her grandson Claude dearly, so she might have told him."

"And Alfred Bailey could have told his good friend Sanders Lane," Margo extrapolated. "And the grandson could have told the fiancée. That makes for a lot of suspects. Do you have any idea who inherits?"

"Not at all. Actually, I was planning on having a few words with her, and I would have asked her, for her own sake. That was one crazy stunt that she pulled. I wanted to caution her. But then—suddenly— she collapsed, and the doctor and the servants ushered us out, and that was it. I heard someone say that the ambulance was on its way, and before I knew it, the front door was slammed on our noses. I had no choice but to get in the car and drive back home just like everyone else.

"Anyway, I called her this morning, and she says she's doing fine. She spent a couple of days at the hospital, and was discharged. The doctors think it was a minor heart episode due to the excitement of the party. But I don't know. I'm terribly worried about her, Margo. Something doesn't feel right. I've known her for years, and I'm absolutely sure that an exciting party and a jumping dog wouldn't have been stressful enough to cause her to faint."

"But Father Armand, she's an old lady. Doesn't this kind of stuff happen to old people all the time?"

"I suppose it does. But you weren't there. I'm not an observant man, mind you, but there was an undercurrent of evil in that room. They were all so excessively cheerful." Father Armand shook his head as if he was shaking off the bad feelings. "It was very unpleasant. It was like being in a play, everyone saying lines, but not really meaning them. And then, you should have seen the shock in their eyes when they heard about the will. That's a big house like yours. A well-hidden will could get lost in there for years and years, and all the beneficiaries could die off before they got their inheritance. Someone must have felt that she needed to be stopped fast—before those changes were made— or before the will got lost in that enormous house of hers forever."

"I agree. They would try to act the sooner the better. But, if someone was trying to kill her, they went prepared with the poison in their pockets. So it had to be someone who already knew of her intentions. Someone who had time to get the poison." Father Armand nodded at Margo.

"They're all probably on edge, wondering if they're going to get cut out of the will," he said.

"I'm sure they are. I must say that your friend did a very foolish thing by announcing her intentions. But it would seem that you have nothing to worry about. Perhaps it was really nothing more than a minor heart episode. Didn't the doctors at the hospital say that she was fine?"

"Yes, they did. But would you go see her anyway? I hear that Verdi's *Il Trovatore* will be performed this weekend in Lafayette, at the Heymann Center. Maybe you would allow me to persuade you to accept two tickets as a thank you?"

"Father Armand, you know me too well." Excitement twinkled in Margo's eyes. She loved the Opera. Her mother—the Sublime Nicola Fontaine—had been a famous opera singer back in the day. "Thank you for the thought. I think I can talk Lucy into accompanying me to the Opera. But just so that you know, I would have been more than happy to go see your friend anyway. Now, you said you made me a list of the guests who were at the birthday party, and everything you remember about them."

Chapter 6

The Mutiny

MARGO HATED CONFRONTATION. On principle, she preferred to travel alone, though, in this case, she was happy to bring Lucy on account of the Opera. But Brooks was right. Brooks, the bossy, self-assured young man who was her chauffeur, yardman, and general man-about-the-house, was standing against a column with his arms across his chest.

"Miss Margo, it's not safe to travel alone. The world has become a dangerous place. You have a flat tire and, yes, yes, I know you know how to change it. But there you are, with your back to the road, and someone stops next to your car. And before you know it, you've been kidnapped and murdered, or worse."

"Nothing's going to happen, Brooks."

"No, it isn't, because I'm coming with you."

Brooks wasn't the only angry one. Ice and Fenway, Margo's cats, weren't pleased either. Somehow they always knew when there was an adventure afoot, and they absolutely raised hell if she tried to leave them out of it. They were growling menacingly under their breath.

"I don't understand why we have to make such a big deal out of this. It's just for one weekend," Margo told the hostile room.

"I don't like it that you and Lucy might be in danger, and I won't be there to protect you. Besides, look at the cats." Brooks pointed at the recalcitrant felines. Ice's tail was swooshing aggressively from side to side. "They don't want to stay here with me. They want to be with you."

"Guys, we've been arguing about this for an hour, and we're getting nowhere. Let's do the following. Brooks, if you can find a hotel in Lafayette that takes cats, you can all go. Tell them we need a suite of rooms for Lucy and me, and an adjoining room for you."

"Yes, Miss Margo," Brooks said, grinning from ear to ear, showing his perfect teeth. His good looking face always lit up when he got his way.

"And you, Lucy, find us something nice to wear to the Opera."

"Yes, Miss."

"Okay then, dismissed everyone."

Everyone scattered happily. Even those rascal cats were content now, purring shamelessly on the sofa. Margo slowly took the steps up the ample staircase, passing her fingers across the exquisitely carved banister as she went. What opulence. If her mother could see her now, what would she say? Would she be proud of her mousey daughter for managing to recover the estate, complete with home and fortune? Even after her mother's death, even after achieving all this, Margo couldn't overcome her sense of inferiority whenever she thought about her, so beautiful, so famous and so glamorous.

She walked to her bedroom, carefully avoiding stepping on construction material. Remodeling was an ongoing project. The big bedroom she picked to sleep in was a trip through memory lane. From over the fireplace mantel, dozens of photographs stared at her from sepia and black-and-white frozen moments. She knew none of these people. They were probably her relatives, lost and gone. But never mind, she wasn't going to put them away. She loved looking at them, admiring the old classic cars, the frilly hats and the button-up boots. A couple of them had horse-drawn carriages in the background, reminding the world of their back-breaking existence. There were only two photographs in color. One was of Margo and her mom, smiling happily at the photographer taking the picture, and the other one was of her mom after singing Bizet's *Carmen* at the Met—at last curtain—receiving an enormous bouquet of roses, smiling at the adoring audience.

She heard Lucy singing to herself, rummaging around the armoires in the guests rooms among the beautiful party clothes left behind by her ancestors. She didn't have a thing to worry about. Lucy's experience as a stage seamstress, and her impeccable good taste, always ensured that Margo was appropriately dressed for every occasion. Besides, if something didn't fit properly, Lucy could fix it in a very short time. "I also need something to wear to afternoon tea in a sun-room," she told Lucy in passing.

While Brooks drove and Lucy chatted about important yet oddly inconsequential things, Margo and the cats slept in the back seat of the Mercedes, lulled by the quiet purring of the expensive engine and the warmth of the chenille throws that covered them. When they reached the tall and impressive bridge over the Mississippi River in Baton Rouge, Lucy woke Margo up so she could admire the view, and after that, she remained awake.

The massive steel truss bridge rose from the darkness of the early morning sky like a portal to another world. Visible from far away, it loomed menacingly high up in clouds that were slowly being tinged with the pinks and yellows of the rising sun.

Soon, they were driving up at its highest point. From that dizzying height, Margo could see the wide muddy river crowded with ships and barges of all sizes. Enormous factories stretched on the edge of the river all the way to the end of the horizon, and their numerous smoke stacks spewed into the air a continuous flow of ugly, dark, greenhouse poison that billowed in the foggy morning even at this early hour. It could have been a lovely sight with the river at her feet and an open vista that extended for miles on each side. But, the pervasive industrialization of the river bank gave it the appearance of a dirty, overworked town.

For the next hour or so, Margo watched the hypnotic early-dawn alien landscape of the Louisiana swamps, with the trees growing right out of the water, and big, heavy birds flapping among their branches. They drove through an endless bridge that crossed the swampy water for miles and miles. She watched for alligators, but the car was going too fast. Someone had told her that the Atchafalaya Basin was full of alligators, but who knew if it was true.

After the recent rains, the muddy, chocolate colored water was too high for comfort. In an oddly claustrophobic way, it reached almost to the bridge itself surrounding the seemingly fragile structure, and threatened with swallowing it or sweeping it away. It was not a good feeling. But Brooks was a good driver, and she kept telling herself that there was nothing to worry about.

The sun was coming up now in its full glory, coloring the lower horizon behind them with a splendorous palette of reds and yellows. Nowhere had Margo ever seen riotous sunrises like in Louisiana. The first rays of the sun came tumbling out from behind the lower branches of the cypress trees, coloring the vast river basin like a Matisse painting in all the warm hues of the morning. Here and there, a fishing boat bobbed happily on the water. All you could see from the bridge was a big hat, a rod, and a beer cooler.

The highway deteriorated for a while as they got closer to Lafayette, and finally, the Mercedes got off I-10 and everyone sighed with relief. Two hours plus of being bullied by eighteen-wheelers was a nerve-wracking experience.

The town was still sleeping as they drove through it. Except for a few strip malls and long uninhabited stretches, it was just a small town, a university town. Most buildings were no taller than one or two stories. They passed a few school buses and random people walking their dogs, and finally found an all-night diner open and stopped for breakfast.

After checking in at the hotel, Brooks and the crew dropped Margo off in front of the old plantation home and agreed to pick her up in the afternoon.

Without their GPS, they would have never found the place. The house sat in an oasis of peace and seclusion, right next to a busy street where the cars of morning commuters were already buzzing by at full speed. And yet, in this quiet spot, there was just a dirt road, two enormous houses built way back, and an endless canopy of trees. She rang the doorbell and heard it echo somewhere deep inside the house. It was still quite early.

Chapter 7

Afternoon Tea

THE PLACE LOOKED NEGLECTED, as if the people inside had stopped caring. But the setting itself was magnificent: a ghost of the glory of former times. It definitely had a gothic atmosphere. She took a few steps back to admire in full the enormous three-story antebellum mansion, and the gigantic round Doric columns in the front that helped to hold up a porch framed with a white wrought iron balustrade that was turning greenish with mold and was about to be smothered by an overgrown Virginia Creeper. Dozens of live oak trees graced and shaded the enormous gardens around the house. She could see how someone would commit murder to inherit a place like this, especially if it came with money.

She rang the doorbell again. Finally, she heard the telltale shuffling. That would be the butler. She waited patiently as the footsteps slowly approached the door, and was surprised by the friendly face with big, inquisitive eyes that greeted her. A little man with a deep, mellifluous voice and a heavy French accent: how wonderful, she thought. Margo, who was very in-tune with the sounds and rhythms around her, instantly fell in love with him.

After greeting the extraordinary little guy, Margo handed him her calling card, and he slipped two fingers into his waistcoat pocket and conjured up an old-fashioned monocle, which, like the white rabbit in the Alice in Wonderland story, he put to his eye, and read her name out loud.

"Ah, I knew a Fontaine once," he said dreamily with a heavy French accent. "It was in a magnificent performance of *La Forza Del Destino* at the Met about ten years ago," he added, looking up at her.

"Yes, you must have seen my mom, Nicola Fontaine. She was a famous opera singer," she answered delighted.

She followed him through the cavernous house, watching the methodical way in which he shuffled his feet as he walked. So the butler was a secret opera lover. She giggled to herself.

She admired his outdated butler's uniform. Now that Lucy and Brooks were in her life, she had acquired an appreciation for people who loved to dress up in the clothes of a bygone era. Those two were forever rummaging in the attics for faded vintage clothes, and wearing them for any excuse whatsoever. Perhaps his mistress had offered to buy him more modern clothes, but—like Brooks and Lucy—he had preferred to wear these vintage ones.

As she walked through the dark rooms, the butler gave her the tour.

"The house was built in 1834. The owner sailed to New Haven, and shipped home the carpeting and the furniture. During the Civil War, the house was occupied by Union troops who lived on the first floor. The house was inhabited on and off, and fell into serious disrepair, but was restored completely by John Bingham, Madame's late husband."

Margo followed him quietly around the house. There was a secret pleasure in peeking at other people's lives. It was like voyeurism. She shivered with delight. The main Stair Hall looked like the inside of an English Manor, as seen in old movies. All the doors were carved wood, as were the mouldings, the panels, and the panel tracery. You had to give it to those carpenters of yore. Storms, floods, and hurricanes—as often as they assaulted Louisiana—had never brought this beautiful old building to its knees.

A number of things surprised her when she stepped from the dark house into the sun-room, but the most striking one was that the sun actually managed to shine in. The canopy of trees all around the house made you think that the room would be dark, dank, and gloomy, but not so. The sun shone gloriously in bursts through the branches, and was magnified by all the mirrors and brass objects scattered about the room. There were so many windows all around, that you thought you were in the middle of the forests on a sunny day.

Then there was the décor. Granted, Margo had never been to India, but it suddenly felt like she was there right now. On one side of the spacious room, a plethora of orchids competed for space and attention with other exotic plants. An Indian wall tapestry hung on the wall behind them, featuring elephants with golden tusks.

Two potted orange trees, incongruously full of ripening fruit, stood on the other side of the room behind a large table loaded with tea cakes, and fruits, and sandwiches. The rattan furniture, that palm tree stuff that is woven into thick ropes used to make furniture in so many places in the Orient, looked very authentic, and not like something you could buy at a local store. The batik pillows in floral patterns filled the unexpected room with exuberant color that was oddly pleasing, even if it was so unusual.

The butler stepped through the lintel and announced her formally with his deep melodious voice with as much pomp as if he was announcing the Queen.

Carolyn Bingham-Breaux was exactly the way Father Armand had described her. Soft and fluffy, she was charmingly plump, the way kindly grandmothers should be. She had a mop of curly white hair, pink rouge on her cheeks and lips, and round reading glasses. Her smile was instantly genuine and welcoming. There was no trace of the illness that sent her to the hospital just a few days earlier. When she spoke, she had the faintest trace of a foreign accent.

"Armand just worries about me too much," Carolyn told her after they had gotten the amenities out of the way. "I'm fine. It was a minor heart episode. No reason I shouldn't live another twenty years, the doctor said."

"This is Dr. Schroeder, your friend?"

"No. Dr. Schroeder isn't a practicing physician. He owns a sanitarium for rich people who need to take a few days off of their busy lives, or disappear for a while. No, they took me to the emergency room, and my regular doctor came to check on me. I assure you, there's nothing wrong with me."

"Miss Carolyn, are you aware that Father Armand told me everything that happened?" When the old lady nodded, Margo continued. "It was very imprudent of you to tell your guests about the will."

"I know. I regretted it the moment it came out of my mouth, but I couldn't take my words back." Carolyn looked down, mortified. She was wringing a cloth handkerchief in her hands. "Sometimes I feel disappointed in them, and I have the temptation to write them out of my will. When I see them fuss over me, or visit me and bring me gifts, it hurts to know that it's not because they care about me, but because of my will. Except for Claude. Sweet Claude, he's always been like my own grandson. He's kind and generous, and doesn't have a bad bone in his body. Did Armand tell you? He's my late husband's grandson. I said what I said out of spite, to see how they reacted, but of course I would never have the heart to disown any of them. I know exactly what they are like and ultimately, I accept them the way they are."

"Who inherits? You don't have to give me the details but I would like to have an idea."

"They all do. Benoît, my butler, is getting old. He doesn't have any family. He'll go to a good nursing home where they'll take care of him as long as he lives. Sharmila, the maid, will get a little house I have on the Northside behind the Country Club that has tenants in it at the moment. I'm very pleased with her. She's a decent woman and has taken very good care of me and the household. But she's only been with me a short while, so if I were to die soon, she'd get some money instead, and the house with its tenants would go to Claude for income."

"So basically, the longer you live, the better it will be for Sharmila."

"Exactly. The bulk of the money goes to the young folks, of course. I have to leave it to someone. I never had any children of my own, and now my niece is my only blood relative left. Claude will be well taken care of, though. He's been the light of my old age. I hope to see him married with babies before I die."

"How about the neighbors?"

"They've been pestering me for some of the land. They'll get it."

"The attorney, Alfred Bailey?"

"He's a greedy fool. His wife has all the looks and all the money. I'll be leaving him some money of his own. He's served me and my family well enough all these years."

"How about your three friends?"

"You mean Dolly, Dotty and Renée? You can't be serious. They're too old to want to kill me."

"Do they get anything?"

"Oh, yes, of course they do. They're the best friends I've ever had."

"Do they have any children or close relatives?"

"Yes, all three of them do. Why do you ask?"

"Because their relatives could be interested in your swift demise, knowing that your friends will inherit."

"I never thought about that."

"And that leaves the doctor."

"Ah, yes. Desmond Schroeder. I haven't always been fond of him. Years ago, my husband got sick. Desmond said it was nothing serious, and encouraged John to go spend a week at the sanitarium instead of going to the hospital. I was furious, but they were good friends, and John listened to him instead of me. He was dead within the week. What Desmond Schroeder insisted was a simple indigestion turned out to be a massive heart attack. To make things worse, the medicines they gave him at the sanitarium aggravated his condition and precipitated his death. If he had gone to the hospital instead, he might still be alive."

"That sounds horrible. But you forgave him anyway?"

"Yes. You are too young to know that hatred and grudges fester in the heart, and they do more damage to you than to the person that has wronged you. For my own sake I forgave him. I couldn't continue living with the bitterness that had taken root inside me."

"And he's in the will as well?"

"Yes. Rather, the sanitarium is. He'll get money for better equipment and more qualified personnel. Hopefully, the terrible mistake that killed my husband won't be repeated. As I told you, I can't take the money with me. I have to give it to someone."

"Miss Carolyn, after Father Armand came to visit me, I gave this a lot of thought. I would advise you to get your guests together again, and tell them that you've added a codicil to your will that states that if you get murdered, all your money will go to Animal Welfare. Even if it's not true. It might keep you safe, just in case someone has bad intentions."

Meantime, the foreign maid had quietly stepped into the room, waiting for Margo to stop talking. She turned to Carolyn. "Shrimati, the children just called, and they're on their way." Without waiting for an answer, Sharmila, the maid, left as quietly as she had entered.

THE VANISHING BLOODSTAIN

"Excellent," the old lady said, turning toward Margo, visibly excited. "That way you'll be able to meet them."

"Miss Carolyn, I understand that you're well, and don't feel the need to worry. But would you mind if I looked into this matter anyway? I know Father Armand very well, and I trust his judgment. He might live isolated from the world, but he knows the human heart like only a priest does. Let me take some notes. I have a tiny camera I can take very discreet pictures with. Nobody will notice. I can look into their background without them finding out. It will be a covert operation. If nothing unusual pops up, and you have no further health complaints, we'll close the case."

"There is no need for that, my dear," she said, leaning closer to Margo and patting her hand kindly. "Please let it go. Tell Armand that I appreciate his intentions, but I'm fine. Nobody is trying to hurt me. You'll see for yourself when you meet the children."

Chapter 8
Margo Meets The Relatives

THE CHILDREN TURNED OUT TO BE adults in their thirties. Parvati, the long lost niece, entered the sun-room first. She was a largish, unpleasant young woman who wore garishly colorful hippy-type clothes and excessive costume jewelry, accentuating her foreign origins. Her bracelets jingled annoyingly with a cheap, tinny clink, just like Father Armand had said. Margo could understand Carolyn having to work hard at liking her. She pushed the others to the side so she could enter first. Loud and opinionated, she stepped into the room and right away demanded to know who Margo was, hand on hip.

"Hi, I'm Margo Fontaine. I'm a friend of Father Armand," she said pleasantly. Suspicion flickered in Parvati's unfriendly eyes right away.

"I hope you're not here to ask for donations," she said in a spiteful voice. "We're not in the charity business. You shouldn't bother Auntie at this time. She has better things to do."

After some cajoling from Carolyn, Parvati agreed to be more civil, and plopped herself on a rattan chair as far from Margo as she could. Margo almost laughed out loud because at that moment Benoît the butler shuffled in and solemnly announced the children, who were all there already. Parvati turned around toward the butler's direction as if she was about to make a snide remark, but Carolyn put a soothing hand on her arm and looked at her with a warning in her eyes. It seemed to

Margo that the young woman habitually had unpleasant things to say about others, and Carolyn was stopping her from making fun of the little butler.

Her husband Matt wasn't nearly as imposing as his wife. He was slightly shorter than she, and much more slender. He almost disappeared into his jeans and sweater. He wore what they call Jesus sandals, from which Margo could clearly see dirty feet with overgrown toenails. She suppressed a shudder of disgust and tore her eyes away from the repulsive feet. His thick glasses made his eyes look too large and vacuous. Rather than shy, Margo pegged him as a pushover. Every time his wife told him something in her loud, bossy voice, he cringed. He sat down by his wife obediently and for the most part kept quiet. Margo wondered if he was as harmless as he looked.

Claude, Carolyn's dear grandson, was obviously grand-mère's favorite. Her face lit up and filled with joy when she saw him approach her. At that moment, everyone else ceased to exist for her. He was a very good-looking young man with a clean, casual appearance and tousled dirty-blond hair, fashionably cut. He had a nice height and a nice body. His lean, handsome face was quick to smile, and his deep and pleasant voice probably appealed to females of all age groups. He most assuredly liked what he saw when he looked at himself in a mirror.

He was cordial to Margo right away and made her feel a welcome guest. Margo got the impression that he was already behaving like the lord of the manor. After all, he was that already, in a way. Carolyn would be sure to leave him her treasured house—lock, stock, and barrel. But when he turned to the side, she noticed the receding chin with disappointment. A receding chin is oftentimes a sign of character weakness. Claude took out a cigarette and lighted it without offering anyone a smoke. It was a rude gesture that was another mark against his character. When Carolyn asked him not to smoke, he grumbled under his breath before tossing the cigarette among the potted palms.

All this time, Valeria—the fiancée—sat unobtrusively close to the rattan side-board. She made no effort at being friends with anyone, not even Carolyn, even though she would be part of the family pretty soon. Carolyn made numerous efforts to befriend her, and went out of her way to talk to her and make her feel included. But she basically ignored the older woman's efforts, and sat stony faced and watched everyone with cold, calculating eyes. Eventually, the others just sort of forgot she was there.

Margo was intrigued by this cold, unfeeling woman, wondering what she and Claude saw in each other. She was a pretty girl: small, slender, with the same shade of dirty-blond hair as Claude. She was dressed stylishly in a multicolored silk blouse and a black pencil skirt, and was wearing well-made designer black pumps.

Valeria had chosen to sit by the busy side-board which was so full of colorful stuff that her multicolored blouse melded into the background, making her look like she wasn't there at all. She reminded Margo of a chameleon: a very clever creature who knows how to be inconspicuous. She was observant of everything around her. Her clear, intelligent eyes—unblinking like a reptile's—took everything in, and showed nothing. She watched Parvati recite a story about beaches and suicide cliffs without showing any emotion. A dangerous person.

At some point, Sharmila came into the room, wearing an exotic gold and purple outfit, pushing a cart with an enormous jug of pink lemonade and a mountain-load of edible delights. She poured the drinks into thick large glasses and passed them around. When she turned to Parvati, she mumbled *Priya*, and Parvati smiled at her.

Then, it was time to go. She received a text message from Brooks letting her know that he was at the front of the house. She was glad to leave. She could safely say that the only enjoyable person in the room had been the hostess. The undercurrent of greed and sibling rivalry was unpleasantly obvious, and she wished Carolyn had wanted to pursue the investigation.

Carolyn Bingham-Breaux walked Margo to the door. Margo stepped through the lintel and saw Brooks solemnly standing by the open back door of the Mercedes, proudly wearing his WWII vintage chauffeur's uniform. That Brooks, she smiled to herself. He was something.

Carolyn gave her a big, happy hug. "I do thank you for having come all the way out here to check on an old lady. I have one small question for you, my dear, before you leave. I hope I'm not being indiscreet. Has Armand paid you for your services?"

Margo laughed. She took an embossed gold business-card holder out of her purse and handed over one of her cards. "He tried, but I don't accept money from my friends. He did give me two tickets to the Opera though. He's really worried about you, you know."

Carolyn nodded and smiled. "I know, dear, but as you can see, all is well. I hope it didn't disappoint you to have come all the way here for nothing," she said admiring Margo's elegant business card.

"We'll see, Miss Carolyn. I have a feeling there's more to this case than meets the eye. But I won't argue with you, and I'll let Father Armand know that I found you in good health. Don't forget to call me if you need me." Margo quickly walked to the car and turned around to waive, but Carolyn Bingham-Breaux had already closed the door behind her. For a second, a knot tightened in her chest, but then she brushed the feeling aside and hopped into the waiting car.

Chapter 9

Il Trovatore

MARGO AND LUCY WALKED into the Heymann Performing Arts Center dressed to the nines in classic Victorian evening wear. People had formed little groups in the foyer and were chatting with excited anticipation, sipping wine or champagne, showing themselves off. A long line of gentlemen in tuxedos stood by the bar waiting to be served drinks, discussing important issues while they adjusted their itchy collars and wiggled their feet in uncomfortable but expensive shoes. Margo didn't know anyone in Lafayette, so they went upstairs straight away.

They were escorted to their balcony seats clutching their programs, and they settled down to watch people. Every seat in the house was sold out. This was one of the few stages in America to ever host all three Russian Ballet superstars: Rudolf Nureyev, Mikhail Baryshnikov and Alexander Godunov. And they put on quite a spectacular Nutcracker Suite every year for Christmas with famous ballet dancers from around the world. Quite a feat for such a small town.

The well-dressed crowd was excited, people telling each other hello, or waving from one balcony to the next. The respectful murmurs and the rustling of expensive fabrics as they rub against each other— accompanied by the random tuning of some instrument in the orchestra pit—are almost as exhilarating to the opera lover as is the music itself.

Noises in the orchestra pit announced the arrival of the Concertmaster and the beginning of the official tuning, and the people started heading to their seats after saying quick goodbyes. Then, the lights went out, and the massive curtains swooshed open.

Scene 1 opens with the guard room of the castle of Luna in Zaragoza, Spain. Ferrando, the captain of the guards, orders his men to keep watch over Count di Luna who paces like a caged tiger beneath the windows of Leonora, lady-in-waiting to the Princess. Di Luna loves Leonora and is jealous of his successful rival, the troubadour Manrico.

Suddenly, a group of four latecomers disrupted the performance by shoving their way rudely to their seats, stepping on toes and hems of evening dresses as they went without any consideration. Margo stared down at them angrily like everyone else in the theatre. But suddenly, she realized she knew the four she was watching. She grabbed Lucy's arm and whispered to her, "Look, it's them. It's the people I met this afternoon."

Disregarding multiple shushes from the spectators around her, Margo twisted her body forward and focused her opera glasses on them. They were not as good as regular binoculars, but she could see the four people well enough to notice that they were very chummy, much more than they had been at Carolyn's house. Even Valeria seemed to be grinning. She didn't quite know why, but these four gave her the creeps. She had been asked by Carolyn not to interfere, so she sat back in her seat reluctantly and shelved the unpleasant incident.

Giuseppe Verdi wrote Il Trovatore in 1853, when he was 40 years old, at the height of his fame. As all other operas of its time, the story is twisted, gory, and complicated. The scenery usually includes pits that spout up real fire, as well as a great number of corpses.

Agnes Makóczy

The story begins with a witch unjustly burned at the stake for putting a curse on the infant son of Count di Luna. The baby disappears, and the search party finds the charred remains of a child where the old gypsy had been burned. They assume it's the count's kidnapped son, but the father, Count di Luna, is convinced that his son is alive and never stops looking for him. On his deathbed, the Count makes his elder son swear to continue the search for his younger brother.

In truth, it isn't the Count's infant son who has died. Azucena, the witch's daughter, watched her mother die in agony as she was being burned alive. She screams, "Avenge me, Azucena!" So Azucena abducts the Count's infant son and plans to throw him into the pyre where her mother's embers are still burning. But Azucena is carrying not only the Count's son in her arms, but her own as well, and in the confusion throws the wrong baby into the fire. She then discovers—to her horror—that she has put her own son to death. She decides to raise the Count's boy as her own, and names him Manrico.

Later, as adults, Manrico and the Count's older son don't know each other, but fall in love with the same woman: the beautiful Leonora. Manrico succeeds in winning the young woman's heart, and a lot of confusion ensues at the end of which Leonora sacrifices herself for him by drinking poison. Mad with jealousy, the Count's son orders the execution of Manrico in front of Azucena, his mother. Once Manrico is dead, Azucena cries: *Egli era tuo fratello! Sei vendicata, o madre.* "He was your brother ... You are avenged, oh mother!"

Margo was sighing wistfully at the last notes of the tragic opera, wiping a tear away discreetly, when she noticed Carolyn's four young relatives pushing and shoving again, leaving before the final curtain. Margo itched to follow them and find out what they were up to, but she had been asked not to.

THE VANISHING BLOODSTAIN

All that night and the next day on the way back home to Half Moon Bay, rubbing Ice and Fenway in her lap, she kept thinking about Carolyn Bingham-Breaux, the perfectly lovely old lady with the perfectly unpleasant family, and tried to figure out what it was that bothered her about them so much. But because life goes on, in a few days she forgot all about them.

Chapter 10

Carolyn's Ghosts

CAROLYN SIGHED WITH RELIEF when the last of her guests closed the door behind them. It was becoming harder and harder to lead a double life: sweet and loving grandmother, neighbor, and friend by day, terrified owner of haunted plantation home by night.

Her guests had stayed too long, and she was exhausted. She needed to lie down to stretch her stiff, aching body. Her head was throbbing again tonight. The sharp pain behind her eyes banged in her veins to the rhythm of her steps as she walked toward the staircase.

Sharmila turned the lights off downstairs one by one as she retreated to the servants' quarters in the back of the house, and Carolyn was left all alone in the heavy darkness. She blinked repeatedly, adjusting her eyes to the dark. How she wished that she hadn't sent everyone home, but she couldn't bear their cloying company any longer.

She slowly climbed the endless staircase that led to her second-story bedroom, counting the creaking stairs as she went. Every year it got harder and harder for her old knees to do so much climbing, and she knew she had to face the possibility of moving to one of the bedrooms downstairs. But she was terrified of the downstairs at night. Because—in spite of what everyone thought—there was something down there that came out at night; something that she didn't understand, that slithered about in a foggy miasma during the dark hours of the night, rustling like roaches trapped in a wall.

Carolyn didn't dare sleep downstairs. She knew those ghosts were there for her. They always had been. They had pursued her from country to country across the globe without respite. Some nights, she wished that God would take her already and put her out of her misery. But she was also afraid of dying.

She reached the last rung and refused to look behind her. Once or twice—many years ago—she had dared, and had watched, terrified, the fog rise behind her, and saw the things squirming in it, unspeakable things that made no sense. No, Carolyn didn't look behind her.

She entered her bedroom as fast as she could and locked the door with the old bolt and the new one that Pierre had installed for her recently. She listened with her ear to the door. Her breath was coming in jagged gasps and her hands were shaking. She had a feeling that they were down there, waiting for her, looking upward toward her bedroom door, hoping that she would open it and come out. She wondered—like she did every night—what they would do to her if they ever caught her. As she got older and slower, she also wondered why they never had. Maybe they enjoyed the fear they brought out in her. Maybe they laughed at her as she scrambled with difficulty up the steep rungs of the staircase, and that was all they wanted from her.

She was so tired tonight. Maybe she would be able to fall asleep. She changed into her night gown and climbed in bed with her Bible as she did every single night. Sometimes, the fear was so unbearable that she didn't close her eyes at all until the first rays of the sun came out. Other times, she was too tired to be afraid. Then she fell asleep with the lights on, with the Bible open on her chest. She dearly hoped this would be one of those nights. She started reading fervently.

Then she heard the noises. They had arrived. They were down there. She could hear them whispering, and they were dragging something on the floor. Then, she heard what she had never heard before: the stairs creaking one by one. They had never come upstairs, these ghosts, never in her whole life. But they were tonight. She could hear them. One step, another step, and then another, and her heart was pounding so hard that it was about to jump out of her chest. Please let me die God, please let me die, she prayed, but God didn't need any more dead bodies tonight, and the footsteps kept coming closer and closer.

Carolyn huddled under her quilt, afraid to breathe, afraid to move, and prayed like she never had before. She heard the creaking floorboards in front of her bedroom door, and someone trying the knob. With eyes that couldn't tear themselves away, she stared at the door knob as it turned from side to side. She felt that she was about to lose all self-control and begin screaming like she had never screamed before.

She clutched the Bible to her chest, wondering—mesmerized by the gyrating door knob—what would happen next. But Pierre had done a good job, and the door remained closed. She counted the seconds, frozen in a position of terror, but then she forgot how many she had counted to, because slowly the footsteps retreated, and she heard the creaking of the stairs as her ghosts went back down. Finally, relieved and exhausted, she managed to fall asleep.

Chapter 11

A Month Goes By

IT WAS ALMOST DARK by the time Margo started heading home. She still walked to and from choir rehearsal at St. Quintian's Church whenever she could. The walks provided much needed outdoor exercise, and time for solace and meditation, the kind that is only possible when you're walking the streets on your own.

Street lights were coming on one by one, and the bugs flocked to them right away. House lights were coming on now as well. The little town was hunkering down for the night, around stoves or fireplaces, drinking something to keep warm. A wedge of moon was peeking into the horizon, and strips of clouds slowly sailed by. On nights like these, Margo was at peace with the world.

The air still cooled down at night, and Margo wished she had brought a jacket. Hands shoved in her jeans' pockets, she bent her head against the sea wind that whistled down the street bringing with it the pungent and spicy aroma of Creole food on someone's stove. Her mouth watered remembering she hadn't eaten a bite since lunch, and she picked up her pace.

She loved the twilight. There were still some children playing outside here and there, but for the most part the side streets she walked through were quieting down. Moms were calling their children home to dinner, and dogs were settling down in front of the porches for their nighttime vigil. Once upon a time they had barked at her, but by now they were old friends. Some even wagged their tails at her with some enthusiasm.

She knew it was trouble the moment she stepped through the front door and saw Lucy running recklessly down the stairs. There was some nurse called Mercy on the phone wanting to talk to her, someone from Lafayette. Immediately alert, she remembered Father Armand's old friend Carolyn, and her heart did a somersault hoping that nothing bad had happened to her. What the nurse had to say was garbled and confusing, but finally she got the gist of it.

"Please slow down, Mercy, and start at the beginning."

"Okay, Miss. It was like this. Last week Mrs. Carolyn Bingham-Breaux checked herself into Dr. Schroeder's sanitarium. She came complaining of strange happenings at her home. The furniture was being moved around while she slept. Some of her favorite photographs were missing, and some rug had a bloodstain that had reappeared, and then disappeared, a number of times.

"Her family, and her doctor, and everyone, insisted she was imagining things. Her doctor declared that all that was wrong with her was that she was getting old and senile, and Carolyn got furious with him and refused to talk to him again. But she was already close to a nervous breakdown, so she finally allowed her family to talk her into spending a few weeks at the sanitarium. Just for a good rest, you know."

At this point, Margo got very nervous. She recalled Carolyn mentioning the death of her husband at the hands of the incompetent doctor and his staff. She asked to talk to the old woman.

"She's gone," the nurse said. "Went back home this morning. She said the medicines were making her sick. She had a row with Dr. Schroeder this morning and walked out before anyone could stop her."

"Goodness, did she really walk out?"

"Not walked, no. I called her a taxi. But please don't tell anyone. Dr. Schroeder was furious that she had left."

"Of course I won't tell. Thank you for calling the taxi. But how did you know to call me?"

"Miss Carolyn, she talked about you a lot. She told me you thought there was something fishy going on at her house, and she hadn't wanted to listen to you. She was sorry she sent you away. She showed me your business card. I suggested that she call you, but she didn't want to bother you. So, when she was in the bathroom getting ready to leave, I copied your number down.

"She told me about the dog, and how brokenhearted she was about it. That's when it all started. Things started changing places, and that rug sometimes had blood on it, and sometimes it didn't. I didn't understand that. You can't get bloodstains out of stuff just like that. Then she told me that a young man had died, and it was his blood. The stuff she talked about, it didn't make sense."

"Hold on, Mercy, slow down. What about the dog?"

"Her dog, Mutt. Didn't you know? They found it dead under the bushes in her backyard. She loved that dog. It was like her own child. They sent for the vet, and they came and took it away. It had been dead for a couple of days at least."

"How did the dog die, Mercy? Did she ever say?"

"No, I don't think so, Miss. But it was a few days after she came back from the hospital when she had that heart episode. That's when they told her, and she was terribly sad that she hadn't been there for the poor dog. That's all I remember."

"They must have found it right after I went to visit her, because she never mentioned a dead dog. And then what happened?"

"Well, that's when she started seeing things."

"But she really didn't see things, did she?"

"No. She said she saw that things were being moved, and the blood. But her family is trying to make it look like she was nuts. But she isn't. I've spent a lot of time with her since she got here, and I can tell you, she's as sane as I am, even if the family is trying to show otherwise."

"Mercy, listen. I'm going to take care of a couple of things here at home, and then I'm going to hop in the car as soon as I can and drive over. I should be there before nightfall tomorrow. Do you know if she's home alone?"

"She probably is. Her relatives don't live there. I'll call her."

"Okay, Mercy, call her. If you can, go stay with her until I get there, spend the night if you can. I'll pay you double your fees; just don't leave until I can get there. And close all doors and windows, and don't let anyone in."

"Is she in danger, you think?"

"I don't know. But it would be best if she wasn't left alone. And Mercy, tell her I'm coming back."

Chapter 12

Kate Sonnier, Attorney At Law

MARGO STEPPED INTO THE COOL, air conditioned room that had once been disgraced politician Thomas Sonnier's office and sanctuary. From where she stood, up on the last floor of the second tallest building in New Orleans, she could see most of the city through the wall-to-wall lightly tinted window behind what was now his niece Kate Sonnier's desk.

In the background down there, far away, she could see the River Walk, with people strolling—as tiny as ants—pushing miniature strollers, and walking miniature dogs. Cars, buses, and trolleys, came and went busily about their business like features in a model village. The muddy Mississippi river shimmered under the early morning sun, glazing the waters with a shiny, oily patina that almost blinded her. Tug boats and cruise ships bobbed silently on the waters to the rhythm of the waves, heading with determination for destination unknown.

Kate Sonnier had kept all the original furnishings that her disreputable uncle had left behind. The office was plush and decadent with its thick carpeting and expensive artwork on the walls. Its new occupant wasn't as sleek and ruthless as he had been, but was every bit as successful.

Ever since moving to Half Moon Bay, Margo had barely seen her good friend. When she heard the sound of high heels coming from the corridor, she turned around and smiled at her pretty friend. Kate hadn't changed much. Her hair was maybe a little shorter, but she still sported that businesslike blonde bob. And she was still wearing her dad's gold watch: the only thing she owned to remember him by.

The girls hugged and exchanged gossip for a couple of minutes, but Margo was in a hurry, so they got to the point.

"What's going on?" Kate asked. "Is this about Father Armand's friend?"

"Yes. She's an old lady, an old parishioner of his from when he was living in Lafayette. She got sick during her 80th birthday party, and her doctor said it was nothing more than a minor heart episode, and after a long weekend of observations at the hospital, she was sent home. Father Armand was present and saw it when it happened, and he thought there was something fishy going on.

"I went to visit her right away at his request, but the old lady said she was fine and didn't need any help. So that was that. But last night, out of the blue, a nurse called me and told me she had checked herself into the sanitarium where the nurse works, due to emotional exhaustion. Apparently, strange things have been happening in the house, things that can't be explained.

"Meantime, her dog was found dead under the bushes while she was at the hospital the first time, and that helped push her over the edge. All in all, it's a bizarre story. I've met some of the people in her life, and I didn't like them. I'm with Father Armand on this. There's something fishy going on.

"Anyway, I have a funny question. Could they be trying to declare her incompetent? Is that something that's easy to do? There's a lot of money and property involved. And she foolishly told them that she was going to change her will. One of them might feel motivated to put her away or have her declared incompetent before that happens. What do you think?"

"Well, that's not so easy to do. They have to file a form before the Probate Court. Then, incompetency must be proven. Usually, two doctors will conduct a psychological evaluation to determine mental capacity. More papers need to be filed. After all that has been taken care of, the Probate Court will determine whether the subject is incompetent or not. They will also determine whether the person who wants to be appointed guardian is suitable."

"Good. It sounds complicated. I might have time to solve this conundrum before they get rid of her."

"You will take care of yourself?"

"You know I will."

"And you will take your gun?"

"Of course. Always."

Chapter 13
Margo To The Rescue

MARGO DROVE UP the circular driveway of her own seaside Half Moon Bay home and walked briskly to the front door enjoying the crunch of the crushed oyster shells under her feet. It had been two years since she'd recovered the family home, but still she hadn't gotten over the awe of living in such a beautiful place.

She assembled the crew and gave them one hour to get ready for departure. Lucy was excellent at this. In one hour she could pack both her and Margo's suitcases to perfection, and, between her and Brooks, they closed down the enormous house, battened the hatches, packed the cats' paraphernalia, and were ready to leave. Before Margo started heading for the front door, the car had already been to the gas station, the tank filled with gasoline, the tire pressure checked, and Brooks dressed in an Edwardian chauffeur's uniform he found in one of the attic armoires, standing by the open back door of the Mercedes, ready to help her get in.

Just to make sure, she checked that the Glock pistol was safely in her purse next to her permit. There was plenty of extra ammo for it in the suitcase. Now that she actually knew how to shoot her pistol, it made her feel safer.

"Lucy, you'll stay with me and the cats in the big house. I have no idea what to expect. This might be a cold run, but you never know. We might have to fight off intruders, so you'll have to be brave. Ice and

Fenway will patrol the house at night. They're smart enough to wake us up if there's anything out of the ordinary." Ice said meow, and Margo continued.

"Brooks, there's a nice guest house out back. I hate to leave you out there on your own, but we need someone keeping an eye on the house from the outside. Sleep in the daytime and keep guard at night. Take photographs of everything that moves. Wear those nice night-vision goggles I got you."

"Yes, Miss Margo."

"And guys, we have at the most three weeks to solve this case. After that, the choir will be back in session, and if I'm not there to sing my solo, I'm going to be in big trouble."

Chapter 14

Mercy And The Bloody Rug

MERCY, SOLID, MIDDLE-AGED and competent, stared down at the bloodstained rug and shook her head in disbelief. The dark spot was pretty big, like maybe two feet in diameter, and it looked suspiciously moist. Benoît had gone pale and was shaking mildly, and Carolyn looked like she was about to cry. Mercy thought about these two harmless old folks, and anger filled her heart. Shame on whoever was playing tricks on these two.

"I told you, Mercy," Carolyn told her pointing at the offending rug. "The bloodstain keeps coming back. And it even looks fresh. Look at it. I told you I wasn't becoming senile."

Mercy—being a nurse—knew all too well what blood smelled like, and besides she was young enough to bend down that far. She knelt down on the clean side of the rug, leaned over the moist mess and stuck her nose to the bloodstain and sniffed. "Yes, it does smell faintly like blood."

"Yesterday there was no stain on it. Remember I showed you when you got here?" Carolyn looked defeated. She kept twisting and pulling the little handkerchief in her hands. It was about to tear.

"I do remember," Mercy said, trying to think. "That was the first thing you showed me. But there has to be a reasonable explanation. Bloodstains don't just appear and disappear like that."

She lifted one side of the rug, and then the others, one by one. Where most of the stain was, the blood had penetrated and seeped through to the backside of the rug and looked almost black. A moist spot was smeared on the floor beneath it, and Mercy bent down again and touched it with her fingertips. "Blood," was all she said.

Benoît was visibly distressed. He had taken his monocle out of his waistcoat pocket and perched it on the tip of his nose. Bent down as far as he could go, he stared at it too, puzzled about the return of the stain.

"It only comes back when you're home, Madame," he told Carolyn. "I don't understand. All this week that you were gone, it was as clean as a whistle. I made sure and checked every day."

Carolyn looked like she wanted to say something, but was too afraid to do so. The moisture of the held back tears fogged up her little round glasses, and she took them off to clean them with her wrinkled handkerchief. There was a lot of fear in those red rimmed eyes. Benoît tried to look brave and nonchalant, but Mercy could tell he was frightened as well.

"Come on, guys," Mercy told them, as she put her arms around shaking shoulders and gently led them to the cheerful sun-room. "Let's go sit down and have something to drink. I'll get the maid."

Chapter 15

Settling In

MARGO AND HER CREW were received with fanfare, like old friends. Benoît—the butler—opened the door for them, but Carolyn, hearing that they had arrived, was already heading in their direction all excited. Mercy—the nurse who had alerted Margo about Carolyn's visit to the sanitarium—peeked out from behind Carolyn's comfortably ample frame with a big smile and introduced herself. Even Sharmila came out to the foyer to say hello. It was obvious that everyone was not only happy but relieved by the arrival of reinforcements.

Carolyn was delighted to be surrounded by so many young people. Her eyes lit up, and her cheeks flushed. She wanted to feed everybody right away including the cats and insisted they follow her to the kitchen where a late table had been set for them, and where the cook was busy stirring something on the stove that smelled like heaven.

A bottle was uncorked, and wine glasses were passed around. You would have thought this was a celebration, and not a murder attempt investigation. The home-made bread came out steaming hot from the oven, and while they waited for their étouffée to be served, they all buttered their bread and gratefully drank up the wine. Brooks—who was going to stay up at night—discreetly passed his wine to Lucy, who didn't mind one bit and drank it all.

THE VANISHING BLOODSTAIN

The cook had set aside some of the shrimp from the étouffée for the cats, and Margo stopped worrying about them anymore. If this was a household that loved animals, the cats wouldn't go wanting.

After dinner, the cook put up a pot of coffee, and Margo and the nurse discreetly moved to the side to exchange information. One of the relatives had shown up in the early afternoon and became rather upset when informed that Carolyn wouldn't receive anyone—nor would she need any help, but remained civil. Margo and Mercy figured the word would spread, sparing them the need to explain themselves. At least everyone knew now that Carolyn wasn't home alone anymore and wouldn't be an easy target. Mercy also filled Margo in about the reappearance of the bloodstain. As far as Mercy knew, Sharmila had dragged the rug to the kitchen with the cook's help and was in the process of washing it. As promised, Margo paid her well, and the nurse left after the coffee and wished them all good luck.

Ice and Fenway—Margo's beautiful cats—were intrigued by the little butler from the moment they met him. He told them hello with his deep, melodious voice and his French accent, and the cats stared at him in wonder. They followed him wherever he went. Benoît—the butler—finally finding that someone was interested in what he had to say, talked to them at large. He was one of those people who talk to animals, and he gave them a tour of the house. Ice and Fenway were used to being talked to and knew how to look attentive. They went from room to room, and the little butler showed them the features of the house, and where they were going to be fed, and how to go outside to the little enclosed inner patio, where they could safely use the bathroom, through the trapdoor that had been built in for Mutt. Sometimes, Ice told him meow, and Benoît answered as if he had understood.

It was perfect. It was the first time on one of their cases that Ice and Fenway were so welcome, and Margo knew they were going to have a good time roaming the enormous house. Even the butler seemed to have become younger and more alert. He shuffled his feet with more enthusiasm. He must have been secretly a cat lover. And then again, Ice and Fenway were so pretty and so polite that it was hard for anyone not to fall in love with them.

Eventually, the excitement died down, and they all retired for the night. Margo sat in an armchair in the dark and quiet living room, giving everyone time to settle down. Sharmila had left a light on outside, above the front door: a yellow one to repel bugs, she said, but the bugs danced greedily around it anyway. From where she sat, she could see through the cathedral windows some of the front of the house and a small darkish patch of the dirt road enveloped in the incoming fog, barely illuminated by the weak yellow light. This house was in a very desolate place. The neighbors were too far away. What during the daytime was old fashioned charm, at night was downright scary. She doubted she would have the courage to live all the way out here all alone.

Some lights twinkled on and off far away between the bushes of the empty lot on the other side of the dirt road. The lights on the busy Kaliste Saloom Road perpendicular to Old Plantation Road were too far to be seen, but occasionally the raucous siren of a police car, or an ambulance rushing by, filtered through the quiet and the fog to where she sat. It would be quite easy for someone to hide out there and wait for the house to settle down. Then, easy as pie, pick the lock or use a copy of the key, and slip in unnoticed. With Sharmila, Benoît, and the cook, way in the back of the house in the servants' quarters, and a hard-of-hearing 80 year old upstairs, they could come and go as they pleased and nobody would ever know. Especially now that there was no dog to greet them barking. It was awfully convenient that the dog was dead.

It had been a long day, and Margo fought back the exhaustion. She watched the mailbox all the way out by the chicken wire fence. A lonesome cat sat on it—still as a statue—and stared right back at her as if it could see her. Behind the silhouette of the cat, a wedge of moon was slowly creeping up in the sky, brightening the strips of clouds that sailed by lazily behind it. Slowly, the floorboards upstairs stopped squeaking, and the household went to sleep.

Margo walked around the upstairs checking window locks and peeked into Carolyn's room—left unlocked during their stay so they could keep an eye on her. Her gentle snoring told her that she was fast asleep already, probably with the help of sleeping pills, or the comforting knowledge that she wasn't alone tonight. She closed the door quietly. She and Lucy would sleep in the first rooms after the landing, across from each other. If someone came upstairs uninvited, the creaking floorboards of the rickety old stairs would surely wake one of them up. They would sleep with their door ajar, Margo with Grandmother's Glock, and Lucy with a baseball bat. She stuck her head into Lucy's room. She was reading in bed with the cats sprawled around her. She waved hello. Then, Margo headed downstairs.

Chapter 16
Tall, Dark, And Handsome

THIS WAS A CONFOUNDEDLY CONFUSING OLD HOUSE, with too many little rooms and stairs and hallways that led here, and there, and nowhere. When she entered the living room, she encountered a tall young man she'd never seen before. Courteous, dark haired with intense eyes, he introduced himself as Pierre, the chauffeur.

"Hi, Pierre, you really startled me. I didn't know there was anyone else in the house."

"Sorry about that," he told her with a sheepish grin. "I thought everyone had gone to sleep."

"My name's Margo Fontaine, Private Detective." She stuck her hand out to shake his. "Funny, I thought the same thing. I came down to check on the doors and windows to make sure they were secure. Do you always walk around barefoot in the dark?"

Pierre looked at his feet self-consciously and shrugged. "Yes, sometimes. I was about to go to bed, but I wanted to check on the doors and windows one last time. Now that we don't have Mutt with us anymore, I'm more careful." Pierre sighed loudly and looked sadly at Margo. "Mutt was the dog. He died a few weeks ago." His voice broke, and then he added softly, "he was my friend."

"I know. I heard. I'm so sorry." Margo put a hand out and touched Pierre's arm. She understood the pain of death all too well. They both looked down awkwardly for a few seconds, and then Margo told him, "It's getting late. We better finish checking those doors and windows."

"This place is too deserted at night," Pierre told her in case she hadn't noticed. "Since Hurricane Katrina there has been a tremendous rise in crime," he added as they walked through the cavernous house turning on lights, checking windows, and then turning lights back off. "We have to make sure nobody can sneak in through an unlocked door or window in the middle of night. This house is full of valuables."

"But everything's insured, right?"

"I don't know. I'm sure it is. But still, it would scare Carolyn or the poor old Benoît to death."

"So you do this every night?"

"Only lately. This used to be Benoît's job, but ever since Carolyn went to the hospital, he's been kind of shaken, so I've taken over for him. Besides, he can barely reach some of these latches anymore." He laughed pleasantly. "I like Benoît a whole lot. Did you know that when he was young, he was in the French Foreign Legion? He was wounded in the Battle of Diên Biên Phu in Vietnam and again in the Battle of Algiers. They awarded him the French citizenship under a provision known as 'Français par le sang versé' or French by spilled blood. You'll have to ask him to tell you some of his stories."

Margo and Pierre walked companionably toward the back of the house. The place was as secure as it could be. But they were both enjoying the conversation and the company, and seemed in no hurry to tell each other good night. Pierre leaned against the refrigerator and Margo against the stove.

"Does it bother you that I ask so many questions?" Margo asked him with an inquisitive smile.

"Not at all. Ask away."

"Do you live here?" she asked and grinned. "I have to ask."

Pierre laughed his pleasant laugh. "I live out back in the guest house, but right now I'm bunking with Benoît temporarily to give your friend space to do his surveillance."

"My chauffeur, Brooks," she specified and nodded. "Have you ever seen any suspicious lights come on in the house at night?"

"Yes, occasionally, I mean not suspicious at all. Sometimes lights come on for a while during the night, but it's probably the people in the house making a trip to the bathroom or the kitchen, just like everyone does sometimes. If there'd ever been a break-in, someone would have told me."

"How about suspicious cars in the driveway at night?"

"I can't see the driveway from the guest house. But if I was an intruder, I would almost have to drive up without lights to the end of the dirt road and leave the car at the dead end. It would be impossible to leave the car on the main street out on Kaliste Saloom where all the traffic flows. There's no place to park, I don't think."

"And Mutt would surely have barked if someone had tried to break in, right?" Margo asked, hating to bring the dog up again.

"I don't know." Pierre shook his head sadly. "He was a friendly dog, and maybe he would have wagged his tail and showed the intruder where Carolyn keeps the silver."

"Well, thank you Pierre. It's really getting late. We better go to bed."

"Good night, Margo Fontaine," he said and gave her a big smile. "See you tomorrow."

Margo watched him go toward the back of the house suspiciously. Pierre was a friendly guy and gave straight-forward answers, but she just had the strongest feeling that he was hiding something. And she wanted to know really badly what it was. Still, he was awfully charming, and she couldn't help but smile.

THE VANISHING BLOODSTAIN

She turned toward the kitchen sink and looked through the glass into the foggy night toward the back of the yard trying to penetrate the penumbra, but the window only reflected back the image of an exhausted Margo with rumpled clothes and disheveled hair. If it was daylight, she would be able to see the guest house perfectly from there, but now there was only the total darkness of a humid, foggy night. She flicked the lights on and off twice and Brooks, who was already on guard, flicked his on and off twice as well. Reassured that he was watching, Margo went upstairs and got in bed.

Chapter 17

Sunday - The Garden Party

THE HOUSEHOLD WOKE UP in a festive mood. Margo followed the aroma of fresh coffee to the kitchen and found everyone around the table already, chatting about the upcoming party, and eating breakfast.

"Miss Margo," Lucy said all excited, "these biscuits and gravy are incredible." Margo sat down next to her and accepted a piping hot cup of coffee from the cook.

"Miss Carolyn," she said, "I thought ladies of grand houses like this one ate in formal breakfast rooms."

"I usually do, but today I couldn't stand the idea of eating by myself. We've been discussing the party at the Country Club."

"Have you thought some more about the changes to the will?"

"I have thought about it a lot," she said, fidgeting with her fork, pushing her food around the plate. "You're right, of course. I'm old, but I want to keep on living. So I'll tell them that if I die murdered, all my money will go to Animal Welfare." Carolyn looked up from her food quickly and glanced at her employees with worry.

Margo could sense that Carolyn really wanted to reassure Benoît and the others—especially Benoît who she was very fond of—that they would be taken care of, but it had been the plan that she should stand firm. She watched the cook frown unpleasantly, and Pierre shrugged, but Sharmila and Benoît almost took no notice. There was a good chance they knew the truth already.

Someone had put a rug in front of the fireplace where Ice and Fenway sprawled, keeping toasty warm. The cook plopped a large glass of freshly-squeezed orange juice in front of her, and a plate of enticingly hot biscuits and gravy with an offended grunt, and Brooks got up from the table, ready to go. He grabbed the grumpy cook by the waist playfully with one arm and threatened to give her a thank you kiss for the wonderful breakfast, to which she picked up the wooden spoon angrily and told him *Je vas te passe une calotte*, and he laughed. Then, he said a regretful good-bye to all and left by the back door.

"He's going to sleep so that he can keep guard over the house at night," she told the others unnecessarily. "So anyway, who's organizing the party?"

"Oh, it was Dolly and Dotty's idea. Not that they need an excuse for a party." Carolyn laughed pleasantly. "When they found out that I was back from the sanitarium, they decided that we had to celebrate. You're going to think, Margo, that we party all the time. And you're absolutely right. But life is too short not to be enjoyed." And with that, Carolyn shoved another forkful of food in her mouth and grinned at her guest.

On the way to the Country Club, Carolyn and Margo sat in the back seat while the chauffeur drove. Like the main street of every other town she'd ever driven through, Johnston Street delivered an unassuming display of car-washes, diners, and pizza places. After a while, Pierre swung left to a side street and drove in front of St. John's Cathedral, Father Armand's old parish, where Carolyn and all her friends still went to Mass. While Pierre gave her the city tour with commentary, Margo watched him from the corner of her eyes. He spoke like a cultured man. He was obviously well-read, as he freely quoted obscure Louisiana history books. His behavior seemed above board. Still, there was something off about him, something she couldn't put her finger on. Occasionally, he looked in the rearview mirror and their eyes met, making Margo blush in spite of herself. Then he would quickly look away.

The Country Club was an elegant building of glass and steel that looks out over expansive rolling hills and park-like walkways. The interior was large, luxurious, and reeked of expensive comfort. Two doormen in uniform opened the glass entrance doors for them, and Margo's eyes popped open with delight. She was in an atrium that spanned three stories in an open-design main hall sparsely furnished with the occasional groupings of white leather sofas and couches, and modern glass and chrome tables. There seemed to be no ceiling but the open sky. Other than the few obligatory birds that flew lazily overhead, the clear blue above her was perfectly empty of clouds and poured its dazzling noon-time light into the sumptuous white room.

Thousands of tiny chandelier light bulbs in large crystal and brass wall lamps further illuminated the enormous hall. The glass tables were topped with ashtrays, and magazines, and extravagant flower arrangements. Paintings on the wall—highlighted by elaborately carved, gold-leafed wooden frames—were obviously originals and portrayed the ever popular landscapes populated with sheep, and farmers, and ox-driven, hay-laden carts. In one word, the walls dripped money. Oil and sugar cane money, and a lot of it. People dressed in their Sunday best were pouring in from the front door. The church crowd had arrived.

They followed the sound of a chamber orchestra playing Franz Lehár waltzes for a while, and went up a few marble steps. The restaurant was to their left, and waitresses were receiving coats and ushering the guests to the buffet beyond. You could smell Cajun Cuisine all the way out to the foyer. Margo turned instinctively toward the food, but Pierre grabbed her arm and pulled her gently in the other direction, toward the back door and the gardens.

In the end, Margo was happy they were seated outside. The day was too pretty to be indoors anyway, and everyone was enjoying the sun and the gentle humidity. Margo—who had absolutely loathed the humidity when she'd first arrived to Louisiana—now loved the way it moistened her skin and gave her hair a cascade of natural curls. A pond fountain behind the seated guests was spouting a froth of water from the mouth of a copper frog. It sprayed up into the air and gurgled as it plopped back into the pond, spreading out in little tight waves, filling the air around it with a mist of tiny water drops. Ducks bobbed on the water, oblivious of the humans around them. There was probably no duck on the menu that day.

Margo had wanted to get to the club before the others so she could observe them arrive at leisure. But, by the time they walked to the back of the club house, a huge gathering of people was already seated at an outdoors table that had been placed there on the veranda for the occasion. Carolyn walked leaning on Pierre's arm and smiled as her friends and relatives jumped up and gathered around her to welcome her to the party.

These older women, they seemed to favor young drivers, she thought to herself. Both Dotty and Renée's chauffeurs were also handsome and young, obviously easy to recognize because they were standing close to the old ladies, wearing impeccable drivers' uniforms. Was she going to be like that when she got old, would she have a handsome young chauffeur, or would she be more discreet like Dolly, who didn't seem to have one?

Margo said hello to the younger folks whom she had already met on her previous trip, and who stared back at her with hostility, and focused on the others. From Father Armand's description, they would be easy to recognize. There was the attorney—Alfred Bailey—with his pretty younger wife Lila. Much younger, Margo corrected herself. They were very well dressed, both of them, expensive clothes, lots of jewelry on Lila, and the real kind too. They must have cost a fortune. Alfred was busy drinking. He didn't seem to be in a very good mood. From his slurry hello, Margo figured he'd already had one or two drinks, big ones. She remembered Father Armand mentioning that he was fond of margaritas. She made a mental note to check on their finances. Lila gave her a welcome smile and waved. At least she seemed nice.

Dr. Schroeder, whom she recognized because he was the only older man, was talking animatedly out by the fountain with Claude, who had barely turned around and waived to her dismissively when she said hello. The doctor looked at her briefly and gave her a quick perfunctory smile and then continued talking to Claude. Judging by their body language, they seemed to be deep in some sort of intensely belligerent conversation. Dr. Schroeder was offering him a cigarette on the sly. They both turned toward Carolyn and looked at her furtively before lighting up. She remembered that Carolyn didn't like young Claude to smoke.

"Oakbourne Country Club was once the Oakbourne Plantation." Carolyn was reminiscing. "It belonged in the Breaux family until 1911, when Colonel Breaux sold it. After many ups and downs, it became a Country Club. My family still holds an honorary membership. My late husband loved playing golf here, and I used to come for Sunday brunch with Dolly, Dotty and Renée, after church."

"Yes," Dolly or Dotty said with a happy gurgle. "We used to hurry up to get here after the service because once the church crowd gets out and gets going, parking becomes impossible. Besides, if you didn't get here soon enough, all the good desserts would be gone." Everyone laughed politely.

"Do you remember we used to rush straight to the dessert tables and grab our favorites to make sure they wouldn't run out?" Dolly or Dotty asked.

"Yes," Dolly or Dotty answered, "and you always picked chocolate pie." The friends giggled. Renée just smiled wanly. It was obvious she wasn't feeling very well. Bernice Schroeder handed her a glass of fruit juice from a decanter and she took some pills. Her skin was pale with a greenish tinge, and Margo remembered noticing how badly she had lagged behind her friends as she had struggled to the gathering with her walker. Her chauffeur had stood guard by her, walking slowly to keep pace with her.

Margo watched Dolly and Dotty have a good time. She was going to have to ask which one was which, or else she would have them confused forever.

"Dolly is the one wearing the brooch, in case you were wondering," a pleasant voice told her as if she was reading her mind and laughed. It was Alfred Bailey's young wife. "She has a ton of them, and I've never seen her not wearing one, ever. She might not have two pennies to rub together, but she does have a lovely collection of them. Hi, my name is Lila."

"Hi. I'm Margo Fontaine, member of church choir by night, and private detective by day." Margo looked at the friendly woman, surprised that she wasn't as snooty and uptight as she expected her to be.

"That's quite a combination. How do you manage to be both?"

"Oh, it's not too hard. I sing in the St. Quintian's Church Choir in Half Moon Bay. I studied music history once and thought about becoming a teacher, but I don't anymore. I find being a private detective much more exciting. And I don't take on too many cases. Only the extraordinary ones, the ones that really intrigue me."

Agnes Makóczy

"Do you mind if I sit down next to you? This is quite a gathering, don't you think? We are all so different, and yet we always end up getting together for some reason or another."

"Yes, it's very interesting to observe the relationships people form in their lifetime. Even if you're all so different, as you say, you all have Carolyn in common."

"Carolyn and her will, you mean."

"True. I did mean that." Ms. Lila was very perceptive, Margo thought to herself.

"Well, Miss Fontaine, what you see in front of you is a bunch of ruthless, greedy people. But Carolyn is an innocent, and she doesn't see it. Look at Parvati, her niece. Nobody knows where she came from. She just appeared one day out of the blue with that weakling of a husband—who is some kind of a psychiatrist, they say—stating that she was Carolyn's niece. She has photographs and birth certificates, but we both know those are easy to forge."

"I'm sure you're right."

"Then, there's that good-for-nothing grandson of hers, Claude. He's always hanging around, waiting for the crumbs she tosses. The things he needs money for always seem so important. He can't wait. He needs them right away. So the old girl takes her checkbook out and gives him some. I don't think he ever asks for too much. He doesn't want to scare her away. But he's always there, needing something."

"But I thought he adored her."

"Just watch him carefully, Miss Fontaine. You'll soon see what he adores about her."

"How about the Lanes? They're the ones in the tennis outfits, right?"

"Yes. They're always wearing tennis outfits. It's rather tedious. I'm sorry, that didn't sound very nice."

"I thought you were friends with the Lanes."

"Not really. They're Alfred's friends, not mine. But I try to be a good wife, so I often tag along. Sometimes, I need to take a break though, and spend some time doing something more constructive. Then, because I love him, I go out with them again."

Margo watched the gathering, enjoying the company of Alfred Bailey's young wife. They both sipped their wines for a while. Then, hoping she wasn't going to alienate Lila with being too inquisite, she decided to ask some more questions.

"That's doctor Schroeder, the older man, right? What's your opinion of him?"

"Oh, doctor Schroeder is a quack, didn't you know? I wouldn't trust him with my hamster. I've always wondered where he went to medical school. Maybe he bought his diploma in some obscure third world country. I don't mean to be petty, but he did kill Carolyn's husband John. He was such a sweetheart. I loved him dearly. And then, he went to the good doctor's sanitarium, and he was dead within the week." Lila looked down sadly at her glass and swirled the wine before she took another sip.

"Yes, I heard. Poor Carolyn."

At that moment Margo saw Valeria pass in front of Renée's chauffeur, and they looked at each other for a second, and then he followed her walk with hungry eyes. Margo—who missed nothing—quietly made notes.

"What do you know about Valeria?" Margo asked.

"Valeria is a mystery to us all. Look at her, how she sits quietly and watches everyone. It's easy to forget that she's there. She just vanishes into the background. I have nothing bad to say about her, except that she makes me feel uncomfortable. She's too quiet. Sometimes I catch her looking at Dolly with a strange intensity, but I have no idea why."

"I wonder if she's in love with Claude. They say they're engaged, but there seems to be no visible affection between them."

"I know," answered Lila. "I've observed that too. I wonder what they're up to."

"And Renée? She's the one with the walker and the ruggedly handsome chauffeur, right?"

"Yes. She's been sick for a while now. I've noticed that her chauffeur is very handsome. But do you know that he always goes everywhere with her? He's very attentive. If she was any younger, I would have to be suspicious."

Both women looked at the handsome chauffeur and then at Renée. She was conversing with the doctor and his fancy wife at one side of the table. Renée was telling them something very earnestly. She looked troubled. She seemed to be trying hard to get her point across. Dr. Schroeder looked angry and uncomfortable, and Margo wished she knew what they were talking about. Renée's chauffeur stood slightly behind her, leaning on an oak tree trunk under its shady fronds. He was chewing on a grass stalk, watching the gathering with interest. He seemed especially interested in Valeria, who had disappeared behind a huge basket of flowers and an oversized bowl of colorful fruit, and sat as quietly as if she wasn't even there.

Carolyn was having a wonderful time. Surrounded by her loved ones and seeing them having fun, she kept putting off the announcement of the will, as if hating to ruin the day. She was telling her guests about her childhood in India.

"Father owned a timber company in upper Burma, which was then part of India. Some of his friends were terrible racists and despised the natives, but not Father. He fell in love with Burmese culture and stayed there for the rest of his life, even after most of the British went back home. He ordered a wife from France, but got one from Louisiana instead—and don't you all dare laugh—she was shipped to Burma like a parcel. They fell in love with each other the moment she stepped off the ship plank, and they remained in love until their death. They had many children, but only I survived, and then many years later my little sister was born."

Everyone listened politely except for Parvati, who was giving Carolyn the most odious look. Matt, her husband, seemed embarrassed and was busy watching his disgusting feet clad in the usual Jesus sandals. Did Carolyn not guess how much her niece despised her?

Her story was very long, and Margo found herself distracted. Her gaze moved around the guests listlessly, watching their reactions, curious about what they were thinking.

At one point, two male club members approached Mrs. Schroeder, the doctor's wife, who was sitting at the far end of the group, and addressed her familiarly. "Hello Bernie, looking good," one of them said with a nasty grin. Bernice Schroeder stood up and took a few steps away from the gathering. The men followed her. She seemed very angry and shook her head and moved her hands a lot, as if rejecting what the two men were telling her. Then the men looked at each other and whispered something Margo didn't hear. They laughed. Bernice Schroeder glared at the men for a second and then walked back to the table. Her face was very red.

The story was taking forever, and Margo wondered when she was going to mention that will already, and she almost got to her feet to whisper a reminder in Carolyn's ear when an unexpected commotion drew everyone's eyes to where Renée had been sitting. For she was sitting no more. She was on her feet holding her throat with both hands, choking and gagging, trying to scream. But the sound that came out of her mouth was an inhuman growl, and it lasted seemingly forever.

Suddenly, people failed to react. Everyone was rooted to the ground—paralyzed—staring at her in horror. Finally, the doctor, who realized he was the one who was supposed to get up and do something, jumped up and ran to her. By then Renée was on the floor convulsing. It was obvious he didn't know what to do. Someone made a 911 call and someone else said that the ambulance was coming. But it was too late. In the blink of an eye she had stopped convulsing, and her bulging eyes, frozen wide open with terror, had gone dull. A thin thread of slime continued to bubble from her lips way after she was gone.

Before they took poor Renée away, Margo approached the body. From where she stood, she could tell that the dead woman's lips had turned slightly blue. The old woman had been poisoned. She was absolutely sure.

Chapter 18

Aftermath

IT WAS TERRIBLE that in the confusion nobody thought to preserve any evidence. The managers of the Country Club, appalled that someone should have had the bad taste to die on the premises, had sent out a mass of waiters who promptly cleaned up every vestige of the horrific event. A small crowd of nosy onlookers had formed around the corpse. There had been so much shoving and pushing, that Margo hadn't manage to rescue either the glass she had been drinking from, or anything else that had belonged to Renée. By the time the paramedics and the police got there, the grounds were so thoroughly trampled down that not even the most efficient forensics detective would have been able to find any clues in the mess.

The paramedics had left with Renée's body already. The way owners, managers, waiters, club members and friends of Renée had milled around in spite of police efforts, all pretense at controlling the scene had evaporated. Margo watched the young policeman talk to the Country Club manager and to Dr. Schroeder, and she walked over to where they were standing to do some eavesdropping if possible.

She soon realized that the policeman's mind was already made up. Renée had been in her 80's and in very bad health. She was under all kinds of medical care, and her death was definitely not unexpected. Just like everyone had assumed that Carolyn suffered a minor heart episode, everyone that had come and gone this afternoon: paramedics, police, and Dr. Schroeder, assumed that Renée had died from natural causes.

Margo approached them tentatively. She knew from experience that her youth and her lack of official credentials often subjected her to derision, and even sometimes ridicule. But, because she knew Dr. Schroeder, she hoped she would get some answers.

"Dr. Schroeder," she asked. "Will there be an autopsy?" Dr. Schroeder looked angry. He grabbed her by the arm and pulled her to the side, not too gently.

"What are you talking about? There's no need for one. We already know what she died of."

"Yes, she was poisoned, like Carolyn was."

"That's nonsense, and you know it. She was a very old woman, and she had a number of health issues. It was her time to go."

"But Dr. Schroeder, surely it wasn't normal for her to convulse like that and grab her throat like she couldn't breathe. And didn't you hear her groan? She was in a lot of pain."

"Miss Fontaine, you're not a doctor. Don't get carried away by your imagination. And please go away. I just lost a patient and a friend, and I have things to take care of. Good day."

Dr. Schroeder turned away irritably from Margo and started walking back in the policeman's direction. She observed the two men exchange a few more words and shake hands. Then, each went on their separate ways. Margo watched them with a sense of defeat: the good old boys' club. She knew well enough how that worked. But never mind. There was more than one way to skin a cat. She walked back to the ruined party.

Carolyn was devastated. She was still sitting in the same chair, her head slumped over her chest, and Margo could hear her simpering. She kept dabbing at her eyes with her small cloth handkerchief. Pierre sat next to her, and his arm was around her shoulders. He was talking to her in a soothing voice, but too softly for others to hear. How ironic that at a party full of loved ones who were going to inherit all your worldly possessions, it was the chauffeur, the only one consoling her. Poor Carolyn. Her loved ones sure were a sorry lot.

She saw Lila sitting by herself at the end of the table. Margo poured herself a glass of red wine and went and sat by her.

"Poor Carolyn. Someone's getting desperate," Lila told her. She was shivering. "She needs to fix that will before someone succeeds in killing her," she added.

"Yes, I agree with you. She's been lucky a second time, but you know what they say."

"Third time is a charm," finished Lila cryptically.

An altercation coming from behind her made Margo turn around. Parvati and Claude were bickering and shoving each other as they walked toward Carolyn's chair.

"You bastard," Parvati was telling him venomously, but as softly as she could, so others wouldn't hear her. "I know why you want to move into the big house. You want to influence her against me."

"Don't be stupid. I just want to make sure she's safe. Someone's trying to kill her."

"Yes. Probably you. You can hardly wait for her to die so you can inherit."

"Well, isn't that what you and your clever, devious Matt are waiting for?" Both the niece and the grandson were up in arms. Parvati tried to shove Claude out of her way as she headed for where Carolyn was sitting. But Claude shoved back.

Parvati turned around and faced the grandson. "If you don't get out of my way this instant," she whispered, "I'm going to tell your grand-mommy what you've been up to. And she's not going to like it."

"What are you talking about?"

"Oh, you know. All the little blackmail games you play. What is she going to think? Do you think she'll disinherit you?"

"You stupid woman. I'll kill you before I let you do that."

Lila and Margo looked at each other, eyes wide open with surprise. "I can't believe Carolyn doesn't notice what's going on around her," Margo said.

"She doesn't want to. That's why. She prefers to think that she lives in a perfect universe, and everyone loves her." Margo just shook her head.

Matt—the husband—picked his steps quickly, trying to keep up with his wife, and possibly keep her from harming someone. When he caught up with her and tried to restrain her, she shoved him to the side with contempt. "Stay out of it, Matt," she told him and kept on going.

Claude got to Carolyn before Parvati did and told her he was moving in with her in a loud, determined voice, and Parvati—right behind him—insisted she was too. But Carolyn refused. She stared at them with sorrow. They continued to argue with her, but Margo could tell that Carolyn was far away, mildly in shock, and was listening to not a word her young relatives said. If she had been slightly mistrustful before, now she looked terrified. The idea of someone wanting her dead had finally been brought home by the death of her dear old friend.

Margo was doing some serious thinking. She still assumed that Carolyn was the intended victim. The four women had freely exchanged wine glasses and tried each other's foods. The poison could have been in her juice or her wine. Renée—thirsty—could have easily reached over and drunk it. Maybe the killer got the glasses wrong, and Renée ended up with the one intended for Carolyn. Maybe, maybe. The point was that the killer had finally managed to kill someone.

"You think someone tried to poison her," Lila asked her unexpectedly. "Don't you? And Renée drank the poison by mistake."

THE VANISHING BLOODSTAIN

It was just uncanny how Lila always seemed to know what she was thinking.

"By the way, have you seen Valeria?"

Lila turned around and looked straight at Margo with big surprised eyes. "You know," she said, "I haven't seen her for the longest time." Margo looked around carefully taking note of the guests. Valeria was nowhere to be seen. As a matter of fact, nor was the dead woman's chauffeur.

Before leaving, the paramedics talked to Carolyn, Dotty, and Dolly, and made sure they were all right, but encouraged them to get in touch with their doctors. Margo had no idea if Dolly or Dotty would. But Carolyn refused to call hers—whom she didn't trust anymore—and determinedly went back to the car leaning on Pierre's steady arm. Before she left, Dr. Schroeder, who always carried a small medical briefcase, pulled out some sleeping pills and put them in Carolyn's hands and encouraged her to take a couple and try to get some rest. And Margo decided that at the first opportunity she was going to take the bottle of pills away from her and have them analyzed. She trusted no-one.

On the way home, Margo tried to console Carolyn, but her tears wouldn't stop flowing. She almost wished she was the one driving and it was Pierre sitting in the back seat with the old woman.

Back at the house, the old dear was made comfortable in her own bed. Ice and Fenway, knowing what to do, jumped up on the bed with her and snuggled.

Ice and Fenway had a soft spot for old folks. Somehow, they knew that purring helped ease the pain, and they purred as loud as they could. Fenway got really close to Carolyn's ear and talked to her softly with her dear little meows.

By and by, the chamomile tea with honey, the purring of the cats, and the gradual darkening of the room as the sun started going down, made the old woman sleepy, and finally she managed to doze off. Lucy sat with her with a book on her lap and a low night light, keeping an eye on her, making sure that her breathing remained even and steady.

Chapter 19
Mutt, The Dog

BEFORE IT GOT COMPLETELY DARK, Margo corralled the maid, Sharmila, and asked her where they had found the dead dog. They walked outside toward the back of the property, behind the house, behind the guest house even, and she showed Margo where Mutt the dog had been found under the bushes by Pierre, who never gave up looking for him.

"Everyone loved Mutt, Miss Margo," Sharmila said with her slight foreign accent, "and we were concerned that he might have run away. Pierre was so worried that every few hours he went out and walked the property all the way to the coulee at the back, calling him. In the end, he found Mutt by the smell. It was terrible." Sharmila passed her hands over her eyes as if trying to get rid of the images behind them. "I hope poor Mutt didn't suffer too much," she said. "It broke Miss Carolyn's heart. She just kept crying. She blamed herself for having left poor Mutt alone when she got taken ill."

"Did Pierre bury Mutt out back?"

"No. We called the vet, and he sent a car to pick Mutt's remains up. That's all I know."

Margo and Sharmila turned back toward the house. The maid walked in silence with her head down. The dead leaves and random tiny twigs left behind from last winter crunched under their feet. The land smelled wet and mildewy.

Agnes Makóczy

The last rays of the sun filtered weakly through the dense foliage, and it was almost dark under the canopy of leaves. It was a quiet and peaceful night, untouched by the noises of the busy city life just a few hundred feet away. The night critters: the raccoons and the possums would be coming out to look for food soon. She hoped that whoever inherited this peaceful place would love it enough to keep it from greedy developers. It was a solace worth preserving.

Then they passed the guest house where Brooks was probably waking up, getting ready for the nighttime vigil, not having any idea of what had just happened. Margo was sure that Carolyn had drunk poison in that champagne glass the day of Father Armand's visit. She was also sure that Mutt had lapped up the poisoned champagne from the floor in his excitement—as dogs often do—and that was what had killed him. This also meant that if Mutt hadn't spilled Carolyn's drink on her 80th birthday, she would be long dead by now.

At the back door, Margo waited for Sharmila to pick off the burrs and tiny dead leaves stuck to the hem of her deep blue and silver salwar kameez, and then they went inside.

That night, for the first time since the escape of five murderers from the Louisiana State Penitentiary in Angola terrorized the inhabitants of Lafayette at least twenty years earlier, all the bolts and all the locks of the house were completely drawn. The inmates had been seen heading south in a stolen car after they carjacked and murdered a cab driver. With relatives in Lafayette, it was speculated that they might turn up in the area. Locksmiths made a fortune during those few days, and the populace didn't leave the safety of their homes until all five inmates were safely recaptured and taken back to jail.

So, on the night of Renée's murder, the inhabitants of Number 2 Old Plantation Road locked themselves up like a garrison, and Margo got in bed with the Glock under her pillow. But not before she and

THE VANISHING BLOODSTAIN

Pierre meticulously checked every door and every window to make sure they were inoperable from the outside.

Margo stayed awake for a long time. She had meant to ask the maid, Sharmila, where she was from, and what she was doing in Lafayette. Not that it mattered this late at night. But it was good to know where all your pawns were stationed. She turned one way and the other, unable to find comfort in the unfamiliar bed. She wondered about Pierre, that quiet young man who walked barefoot around the house at night like a ghost. Who was he? His language and his mannerisms bespoke of someone with a certain level of culture. How and why had he ended up as a chauffeur? Surely, an ambitious and educated young man like him could have done better for himself. Did he have a secret agenda?

Margo was having troubled dreams about handsome young men looking for dead dogs under azalea bushes when she was gently awakened by Fenway's soft paws playing with her eyelids. She sat up immediately in the dead silence and listened. Someone must have trained Ice and Fenway long before she ever met them, because they had this amazing intelligence and know-how to patrol a house and alert her in the middle of the night if something was off. She looked for Ice and saw him perched on the windowsill, looking down. The window was right above the front door and Margo knew he could see part of the walkway and then the mailbox clearly. His snow white fur shone and shimmered like ice crystals in the silvery light coming in from the moonlit sky. He was very still, very focused. When Fenway saw that Margo was awake she jumped off the bed and joined Ice by the window. Their little mouths twitched as if they were talking to each other. Whatever had alerted them was coming from outside—under her window.

The road in front of the house was dark and deserted, and she couldn't see any cars parked anywhere from her vantage point, but she could hear two people whispering right under the window. They were fumbling with the front door lock, fussing at each other. It would have been impossible for them to push the door open because of the metal bar Pierre had placed across the door. This was usually used during heavy storms or hurricanes to keep the doors from banging open. Sometimes the old locks didn't manage to stand up to the fierce winds. Now, Margo was sure glad it was there. She couldn't believe the gall of these people, to try to sneak into the house after a day like that. They must be getting absolutely desperate. She wished Carolyn had said something about the will, but it was too late to commiserate.

She and the cats headed downstairs, careful to not make the floorboards creek. Margo was convinced that it was one of the young couples. She just didn't know which. Unfortunately, by the time she made it downstairs, they were gone. All she could see from the cathedral windows was their backside: a man and a woman. And in the dark, and from so far away, it was impossible to tell who they were.

Chapter 20

Brooks In The Guest House

MARGO WOKE UP WAY BEFORE ANYONE ELSE. She walked to the window and opened it to breathe in the cool morning air. It smelled clean and sharp. The early birds were already chasing worms, chirping in the bushes, and she saw the stray cat from the other night heading off to sleep. It seemed like it was going to be a pretty day. The sun looked plump and bright as it peeked out from behind the horizon. She let the cats sleep a few more minutes while she brushed her teeth and found something warm to wear. This time of the year, the air was still chilly first thing in the morning. Then, she got Ice and Fenway up and told them it was time to get to work.

They passed Lucy's bedroom and found it to be empty. The bed hadn't been slept in. Margo turned back and quietly opened Carolyn's door. The old woman was still sleeping peacefully. Lucy had never left her armchair in the night. She slept leaning against one of its tall wings. Her book had slipped to the floor and her voluminous hair had come out of its up-do and had fallen all over the side of her face. She was snoring quietly. She was going to be very sore today, poor Lucy, after sleeping in such an uncomfortable position. Nobody had asked her to stay with Carolyn all night, but Lucy was a sweet and compassionate girl. And she had taken it upon herself to keep guard over the well-being of the old woman.

Agnes Makóczy

Margo and the cats went quietly downstairs. She had discovered that if you treaded way at the end side of the steps, they barely creaked, so, careful not to step in the middle, they headed downstairs to look around.

The house and its inhabitants were all still asleep. Margo took a quick tour and checked that neither doors nor windows had been breached. When she got to the front door, she faced a dilemma, though. There was the enormous metal bar over the door, barring the entrance. It would have to be a magician's trick to manage to take it off without making an infernal sound.

Then she remembered the famous rug and realized that in the confusion she had forgotten to ask questions about it. She walked to the corner where it was and looked down on it. This was the rug that had sported the famous bloodstain for decades. Lying in a dark corner—in a house full of decaying and aging furniture—it would have blended in with the blues and deep reds of the rug itself and gone unnoticed unless it was pointed out.

But Sharmila had managed to eliminate it altogether. Well, Margo knew for a fact that such a feat was nearly impossible to accomplish, and yet, now that she looked at it closely, she couldn't detect the faintest trace of the bewildering stain. She got down on her palms and knees and examined it closely. Part of it was moist, as if it had been washed recently. She got her face to within an inch of it and smelled. Sniff as hard as she might, she couldn't detect the faintest whiff of blood or of any cleaning product for that matter. She got back up on her feet, satisfied that this rug had never had any blood spilled on it.

She folded the rug lengthwise and struggled it to the door. Then, she unhooked one side of the heavy metal bar and leaned it on the rug, and then unhooked the other side. With this cushioning, at least it didn't clatter as it hit the floor. After she pulled the rug and the bar away from the front door, Margo opened it, and Ice and Fenway bolted outside, frisky at the thought of freedom.

She breathed in happily the amazingly sweet morning air. It was crisp and cool and smelled like ozone. The azaleas were about to open. Clusters of plump multicolored buds covered every inch of the shrubs planted in semi-shade as far as the eye could see. In another day or two, they would open completely and provide a spectacular beauty of such fame that people would come from afar to admire them.

Ice and Fenway ran to the azaleas and sniffed out a good spot to do their business. Then, they quickly washed their faces and their ears and sat down to wait for instructions.

Since moving to the south, Margo had learned that the short-lived blooms rarely last longer than about two weeks. At the same time, azaleas are highly toxic, containing andromedotoxins in both its leaves and nectar. Once upon a time they had been so infamous for their toxicity that to receive a bouquet of their flowers in a black vase was a well-known death threat. She wondered if ingesting andromedotoxins would turn someone's lips blue.

Margo inhaled the fresh air with pleasure. She hoped that someone would wake up soon and make a good pot of coffee. Then, she inspected the area around the entrance. Ice and Fenway were already checking things out, and when she saw them huddled around something and mewling, Margo bent down to look. Someone had flicked a cigarette butt under a shrub to the side of the door. She picked it up with a plastic baggie and inspected it. It smelled fresh, and it didn't look like it had been out there very long. She only knew of one person in the house who smoked, but she would have to confirm that.

Meantime, Ice and Fenway had found something to play with: a small silk flower, completely out of place in a garden full of live ones. They were tossing it playfully from paw to paw, catching it with their nails and tossing it in the air. She had seen such flowers before and tried to remember where. Well, it would come to her. She took it away from the cats and noticed that it was in new condition. She slipped it into another plastic baggie. These cats were better than hunting hounds. They could sniff out clues like nobody else.

They walked around the perimeter to see if something else caught their eyes. Since everything was a dull brown on the ground because of the rotting leaves left behind, she looked for anything that stuck out, anything out of place. After a while she noticed that not fifteen feet from where the first cigarette butt had been found there was a little pile of them next to an oak tree. Margo squatted and looked at them. They sure looked like the other one, same brand, same state of freshness. If she was a betting girl, she would have to assume that young Claude had stood under this tree, leaning against it for a long while. Long enough to smoke all these cigarettes.

They had been smoked to the butt, so he hadn't been too impatient. He had taken his time. But then, he looked like the kind of guy who knew how to pace himself and would take his time. She shuddered. He might have been watching the place, or casing the joint as they say, while he waited for someone. Then he walked to the front of the house and he finished smoking his cigarette, and he tossed the butt close to the flower the other person had lost. And then it hit her: at the garden party. Of course! Similar flowers had been woven into Parvati's hair, unnecessarily she thought, as Parvati was not such a young woman that flowers in her hair would have been admired by anyone. So, Parvati and Claude were the ones that had been there last night, trying to get into the house. Parvati and Claude, *sans* spouses. Why was she not surprised?

The land at the back of the house was still in darkness because the house faced the rising sun. Back there, nature still slept. The air was humid. You could smell the decaying vegetation as you stepped on it, squashing it. There was a light on in the little guest house. Brooks was still awake. Ice and Fenway sauntered behind her, chasing imaginary bugs and getting their morning exercise.

The door opened before she had a chance to knock, and the aroma of freshly brewed coffee came seeping out from the kitchen like a welcome hug.

"Morning, Brooks. Don't tell me you're about to have coffee before going to sleep."

"I can't not have coffee in the morning" he said with a sleepy grin. "Come in, everyone. How are things at the big house? I haven't spoken to anyone since yesterday morning. If I didn't like being alone, I would have gone out of my mind."

"I'm sorry, Brooks. Things were so chaotic last night that I didn't have a chance to come over and get you up to date. But I need coffee first." While Brooks brought the coffee out, she looked around admiring the neatness of the place. It was impeccably furnished and in good repair. A comfortable sitting room with a fireplace and a big flat-screen television opened onto a tiny dining room and a kitchenette. From where she was, she could see Brooks preparing to serve the coffee. An enormous bookshelf chock full of books and knick-knacks made the place look homey and well lived in. "Pierre has a lot of books, did you notice?"

"Yes, and they're very interesting. They are newer editions, so they probably didn't come with the place. There's stuff on physics and chemistry and mathematics. But do sit down. I have some stuff to show you."

"I have a lot to tell you too." Margo settled down in an antique armchair in very good condition that was well padded and extremely comfortable. A Tiffany table lamp next to her looked authentic, as did the artwork on the walls. All this must have come from the big house. Ice and Fenway had decided to inspect the house first and settle down later, and Margo could hear them talking to each other as cats often do.

"There's been a murder. Some friends of Carolyn's had a garden party at the Country Club yesterday afternoon, and right in the middle of it one of her friends got up from her chair, grabbed at her throat and dropped dead."

"Seriously?"

"And I quickly checked on the body before they took her away. Her lips had turned blue."

"So she was poisoned."

"Yes. I tried to rescue the glass that had been in her hands, but you know how curious people get when something gory happens. Suddenly they were everywhere. They were pushing and shoving each other out of the way so they could get close to the dead body. Then, the managers sent the waiters out to clean up everything as quickly as possible, so by the time I managed to fight the crowd, the glasses were all gone. After that, it would have been impossible to find out which one was hers. When everyone left, I tried to look around for clues, but the grass had been trampled down to the mud, and there was nothing left to be found."

"Do you think it was a mix up of glasses, and it was still an attempt on our client?"

"I don't know, Brooks. I'm going to try to find out what the dog died from, but probably it was the same poison that made Carolyn sick and killed her friend. The one thing the two events had in common was that both Carolyn and her friend had grasped at their throats. I'll talk to her, see what she can remember. But I was watching everyone at the party with eagle eyes, and I noticed that Carolyn and her friends drank from each other's glasses and ate off of each other's plates."

"That's the downside to being rich," Brooks concluded. "Your loved ones can hardly wait to see you dead to get to your stuff."

"Indeed. How did you do?"

"Well, there were intruders on the grounds late last night. Came before midnight. I watched a woman use the side gate behind the guest house, and I followed her with my infrared goggles. She vanished in front of the house and stayed there for about twenty minutes. I got as close as I dared. She met up with a guy under the street light, and they went up to the front door and messed with it for a while but couldn't open it. Then, they argued, and left their separate ways. I took some pictures, look."

The pictures Brooks handed her were blurry and rather dark. The guy was muffled up in coat and scarf, but she already knew with almost complete certainty that it had been Claude. Before looking at the pictures she had briefly entertained the thought that it might have been the doctor, who was also a smoker. But this was a slender man. While the doctor wasn't heavy, he wasn't slender either. The woman, she recognized. It was Parvati.

"These are the young relatives. They're hunting for the will."

"They're persistent."

"Yes. They must be getting desperate. By the way Brooks, we'll need to print these out."

"Okay. I'll email them to you. As I was telling you, I found something. I'll be right back."

Brooks came back with a thin pack of letters that he handed to Margo. Some of the envelopes were dated two, three years earlier, but a couple of them were quite recent. They all had the same name on them: Pierre Dubois, and the same sender: Margaret Dubois.

"Did you read them?"

"No. They're in French. You know some French, don't you?"

"Umm, yes, some. Let's see." Margo opened the first letter in the stack and looked at it for a few seconds. "This one says, 'Please don't tell her anything. You're going to make me die of shame.' Or something like that. Let me see this one. 'Have you told her yet?' And then more of the same. They all end with: 'You know how much I love you, Margaret.' Very interesting. Can you take pictures of them and send them to me?"

"Yes, sure. There's another thing. I found no personal items. No photographs, no mail, no bills, nothing. I think he packed everything up and put it away so I wouldn't find it. The letters were under a loose floorboard in the bedroom. But you know how thorough I can be. I found them anyway."

"And he buys good coffee."

"And the guy has an awesome coffee maker. It must have set him back a fortune. You just press a button, and it does everything for you, from the fresh coffee bean grinding to the frothing of the milk. This guy is no ordinary chauffeur."

"No, it doesn't look like it. I'm going to have to have a chat with him."

Margo got up to leave and called Ice and Fenway, but they didn't answer. She looked around and found them in the bedroom by the night table, fussing over a piece of wrinkled shiny paper, tossing it around from paw to paw like a toy ball. She picked it up and smoothed it out.

"Our friend Pierre did leave something behind after all," she told Brooks, who had followed her to the room. "Look. It's a small photograph. A girl with a pretty smile, wearing an unusual breastpin or brooch. Nobody wears those anymore." On the back of there was written the name Maddy and a phone number, a local one: 337-555-5555.

On the way back to the house, Margo quickly went through her to-do list for the day, in no particular order, counting the items on her fingers. 1. Talk to Sharmila about the rug. 2. Find Mutt's vet. 3. Talk to Pierre, but maybe hold on to the letters until they were properly translated. 4. Locate Maddy and 5. Ask Carolyn about the symptoms she felt and a better account on the bloody rug and the impossible stain. It was going to be a very long day.

Chapter 21

Sam Stark

"HI, SAM," MARGO TOLD HER GOOD FRIEND and newly promoted Detective in the Half Moon Bay Police Department. "I hope I'm not calling too early," she told him kindly. She was very fond of Sam Stark.

"Not at all. How are things in Lafayette? Kate told me about your new case, and to expect a call from you."

"Yes, I have a couple of questions. Is there a way you can find out about someone who was born in India? The lady of the house—the one they tried to poison—has a niece that showed up in town out of the blue. She's the right age, but there's something about her that doesn't add up. She tries too hard to be a foreigner."

"Well, Kate said there's a big inheritance involved. We both know what greed does to people. I'll see what I can find out. Email me the details. What else." Good old Sam. Tall, slender, athletic, and very handsome in his uniform, Sam Stark was as kind as he was helpful. He was a throwback to the old-fashioned policeman who would lay his life down for anyone in trouble. Margo imagined him with his little black notebook and his pen, holding the phone with his shoulder and taking notes.

"There's also a greedy grandson by the name of Claude Wilkinson-Cox," she continued. "He's the grandson of her deceased husband. He's too sleek for my taste. He appeared in their lives in his late teens but Carolyn—my client—doesn't know anything about his life before that. Since the husband is deceased, we can't ask him.

"Carolyn told her friends and relatives at her 80th birthday celebration that she was going to change her will, and I'm wondering if they're not trying to off her before she does."

"Do they stand to inherit everything as the will stands now?"

"Yes, they do. Most of it, anyway."

"Is that it?"

"No, Sam. Actually, I was thinking about finding the veterinarian who came and picked up Mutt's body. The dog drank some of the champagne that made Carolyn sick, and he died."

"Poor dog."

"I know. Anyway, I'll try to find out what they did with the remains. Maybe I can have them examined."

"I don't know, Margo. They don't keep dogs in morgues on suspicion of poisoning like they do people. But many pet owners are cruel to their animals, and some veterinarians do look into suspicious deaths and in some cases have managed to bring charges of animal cruelty against them. It's worth a try."

"Thank you, Sam. I'll email you the details. I have to go. I see the maid coming this way. It's my chance to talk to her alone."

Chapter 22

Sharmila

SHARMILA WAS HEADING to the little citrus fruit orchard behind the sun-room with a small basket. Even if Margo hadn't known that she was a foreigner, the way she walked would have given her away. She walked with a tempered dignity rarely seen in American women who are usually in a hurry to get somewhere. Sharmila swayed her hips and took long, elegant steps as she walked to the lemon tree. She was picking lemons when Margo caught up with her.

"Good morning, Sharmila. It's a pretty day, isn't it?" Margo was trying to be friendly, but the woman looked at her with hostility. Margo tried a big smile, and finally Sharmila defrosted some.

"I hope you don't mind, but I would like to ask you some questions."

"I don't have any answers for you, Miss. You might as well not bother asking." Sharmila was done picking fruit and had turned around toward the house.

"Please, Sharmila. I have to find out who tried to hurt Miss Carolyn."

"But I had nothing to do with that."

"I'm sure you didn't, but the more I know about everyone, the better I can fit the pieces of the puzzle together. Do you have a few minutes?" Margo sat down on a garden bench and patted the seat next to her. Finally, Sharmila gave up and sat down reluctantly. She held the little basket of fruit defensively close to her chest.

"How long has Benoît been working here?" Margo took her notebook out and started taking notes.

"He came with Miss Carolyn and her husband when they moved here twenty-something years ago. I think I've heard that he started working for Mr. John when he was a young man."

"What's your opinion of him?"

"He's a nice old man. Quiet. He's deaf, but he can hear well enough when it's convenient for him. He knows more than he tells."

"Does he have any family?"

"I think he was married once. So I've heard. I know why you're asking."

"Why is that?"

"Because of the will. Miss Carolyn is very generous, and we'll all be well taken care of when she dies, but nobody wants her dead."

"Somebody does. Somebody poisoned her champagne."

"I know," Sharmila said with haunted eyes, staring through Margo, remembering something from her past. "People thirst for blood, and when they want something, they don't stop until they get what they came for." Sharmila shook her head as if dispelling unpleasant memories, and her eyes focused back on Margo. "But Benoît is only getting sent to a nursing home. That's no reason to hurt anyone. He's probably older than Miss Carolyn."

"That's true, but others are much younger and stand to benefit more."

"Well, Miss, before you get any ideas, I'll tell you that I will inherit more the longer Shrimati lives."

"Who's Shrimati? Miss Carolyn?"

Sharmila looked startled. "Yes, Miss. I sometimes call her Shrimati. As a sign of respect, you understand? She has been like a mother to me. I lost my mother Jaswinder years ago."

"Where were you born, if I may ask?"

"In Deorala." Sharmila was holding her fruit basket tightly against her chest. She looked distressed.

"Deorala? Where's that?" Curiosity was killing Margo. The pieces of the puzzle were dancing in front of her eyes like saltimbanques refusing to make sense.

"In Sikar. Please don't ask me anymore." Sharmila looked away and stared stubbornly at a clump of lilies.

"I'm sorry, Sharmila," she said, putting her hand on the distressed maid's arm. "I didn't mean to cause you any anxiety. Some easy questions, then."

"No harm done," she said. "I'll answer them if I can. But I want you to know that I'm very fond of Miss Carolyn. She's been very kind to me."

"I noticed that young Claude smokes. Does anyone else in the household smoke?"

"No. Miss Carolyn hates smoking. Only Claude is allowed. Claude is allowed everything."

"You don't sound like you were fond of him."

"He takes advantage of her, but she doesn't notice."

"And Parvati, does she take advantage of Miss Carolyn as well?"

"Oh, no," Sharmila answered, smiling with renewed enthusiasm. "She loves her Auntie and only wants what's best for her." The maid's eyes were shining with affection. "She's a sweet girl."

"Who else lives in the house?"

"Just us two: Benoît and me. Pierre is the chauffeur. He lives in the little house in the back. The cook comes every day and keeps to herself, but sometimes she sleeps here. I don't know anything about her. She doesn't talk to anyone. Sometimes Miss Carolyn tells her what to cook, and sometimes she makes up her own mind. She's been coming for many years. Then there's Maddy."

"Hold on, Sharmila, did you say Maddy?"

"Yes, Maddy, the little maid. She's new. She's been coming for about a year. I can't do everything in the world by myself. This is a big house, and Benoît isn't pulling his weight anymore, so she comes three times a week and cleans the bathrooms and the floors, and does the laundry. She's a nice, quiet girl. Miss Carolyn likes her. Sometimes they play cards together in the sun-room."

"Does this Maddy know Pierre?"

"We all know each other. But Maddy likes Pierre. He's handsome and smart. He'll be a good catch for some girl. She's always looking at him with stars in her eyes."

"Does he like her back?" Margo was thinking about that wrinkled piece of notebook that Ice and Fenway had found in the chauffeur's bedroom.

"No. I don't think so."

"Do you know if Pierre will get anything in the will?"

"That I don't know."

"Okay. Tell me about the neighbors."

"Mr. Sanders and Mrs. Laura Lane?"

"Yes. Do they come and visit a lot?"

"They have visited a lot lately. They annoy Miss Carolyn with all the begging. You wanted to talk about the will. They are going to get all that big piece of land across from the dirt road. That all belongs to Miss Carolyn."

"What do they want that for?"

"I don't know, but I've wondered myself. They want it really badly, too. They look cold and calculating, those two."

"They sure do."

"Miss Margo, I'm going to have to hurry back. The cook is waiting for the lemons." Sharmila got up from the bench and started heading back to the big house. Margo shooed Ice and Fenway off her lap and started walking next to the maid, finding it hard to slow down to her measured pace.

"I understand. Just a few quick questions then, as we walk. Does her lawyer come often?"

"Mr. Bailey? Oh, yes. He wants to be good friends with Miss Carolyn. He brings her gifts and gives her a kiss on the cheeks every time, like they were old friends. I don't like him. He tries too hard. But Shrimati doesn't notice. He's also good friends with the neighbors. I see them a lot, barbecuing in their backyard or playing tennis. The neighbors have a nice tennis court behind their house. I've only seen him with his wife a few times. I don't think she likes the company too much."

"One last question, and then I'll let you go. What about the doctor?"

"What about him? He's a quack."

"Yes, that's what everyone says."

Chapter 23

The Veterinarian

THE VET'S OFFICE WAS NOT twenty miles away across a zigzagging country road. After leaving the house, they turned right on Kaliste Saloom Road, then left at the T, and in barely a few minutes after leaving the busiest part of the city they were already out in the countryside. A two lane blacktop meandered around endless miles of fields, and farms, and random groups of houses that called themselves subdivisions.

The fields of sugarcane had recently been harvested, and they had left behind acres of empty dark earth, scattered with the remnants of drying stalks. Already in some places greenery had sprouted covering the dark dirt with green fuzz. Enormous houses far apart were set back into the horizon. Rich houses that stood watching over the resting land.

On the other side of the narrow road, black and white cows roamed the land waiting patiently for dinnertime. Some lay gathered in the sun as if they were having a conclave, all of them looking in the same direction, while others took over the shady spots under the infrequent trees. A meager coulee provided water to the contented animals and broke the stark grazing land into two in a poetic way. This was the kind of landscape Margo would have loved to paint if she had known how to. A few hundred feet further on, a dilapidated barn kept the hay and the tractor safe. Then there followed more dark empty fields.

Pierre drove in companionable silence giving Margo the chance to observe him. Pierre was—as the song says—tall, dark, and handsome. He was also the brooding sort. He seemed to be a cultured, intelligent man. She instinctively suppressed the urge to like him. There was no proof that he was innocent.

"You have some interesting books in your house," she said, testing the waters. "I hope you don't mind that I checked them out. I'm a book lover myself."

"I don't mind at all. I've always loved to read, but most of those are school books. I'm studying engineering at ULL."

"It must be hard to work for Miss Carolyn and go to school at the same time."

"Not at all. She's a very understanding lady. She knows that's how I pay for my tuition, and she gives me all the free time I need to study. Especially during mid-terms and finals. Of course, now that Benoît is getting old, I do a lot of his chores, but it's still not too hard."

"She does seem like a generous lady. Are you in the will?"

Pierre started laughing. "Wow, you sure know how to get to the point. No, I don't think I'm in it. Why should I?"

"Because Benoît and Sharmila are. I figured she would leave everyone in her life a little something."

"Benoît is more than her butler. He's like a friend. He's been with her for at least twenty years or more. And she seems to have a special bond with Sharmila. I think it's because they were both born in India. But me, at the most she might leave me enough money to finish college, but that's all."

"Thank you for driving me to the vet. I'm very sorry about Mutt," she said, hating to bring the dog up again. "It's probably not easy for you."

THE VANISHING BLOODSTAIN

"I loved that dog, and I hope you find out what happened to him. If he was poisoned, I want to know who did it. We were good friends, Mutt and I, and I miss him. And I'm going to break the nose of whoever hurt him, I swear."

The vet was a small, bald, kindly middle aged man with enormous glasses who liked to talk. Margo braced herself. She didn't really have time to chitchat, but nor could she be rude. She was the one asking the favor, after all.

"So, Dr. Carson, was Mutt poisoned?" Margo asked after the amenities had been settled. Pierre sat in the corner chair with a defensive scowl on his face, arms crossed over his chest.

"Yes, he was. I was going to tell Pierre when he came back for the ashes, but he never did."

"There's been a lot going on in the house. Mutt drank most of the champagne destined for his owner. She barely had a sip, and she was sick for days."

"Well, I can tell you, Miss Fontaine, that the only reason the owner didn't die was that Mutt spilled her drink. It was poison. He died pretty fast. He mustn't have suffered much. We regularly test animals in case of suspicious death. If I hadn't known Mutt and his owner for a long time, and how much he was loved and how well cared for, I would have let the police know. I just assumed that he had guzzled up some of Carolyn's blood pressure medication. He's done that before, you know, Miss Fontaine. About a year ago, he lapped up Carolyn's cough medicine and he threw up."

"And what poison was that, Dr. Carson?"

"Sodium Nitroprusside. It's a cyanide compound: very popular if you want to poison someone. Everyone's heard of cyanide. There's the Tylenol poisonings from about 20 years ago, but you might have been too young to hear about it. Then there was the Jim Jones massacre in Jonestown, back in 1978. More than 900 people died by drinking cyanide-laced drinks. Basically what happens when someone ingests cyanide is that it interferes with the body's ability to get oxygen, and all of the cells become starved for it, and the person dies."

"Is it easy to buy?"

"Unfortunately, yes. If you know where to look on the internet, you can easily buy enough to kill as many people as you want. I wish it wasn't so."

As they were saying their goodbyes, Dr. Carson put a kind hand on Pierre's angry shoulder. "I know how fond you were of Mutt, son. He died within minutes. He didn't suffer long."

When they got back home, Margo saw a number of unfamiliar cars in the driveway: a green dilapidated pickup truck, a couple of older passenger cars and a fancy new one. Margo asked right away who drove the fancy one. "That's Dr. Schroeder's," Pierre answered, pointing at the sleek black model in the driveway. They got out of the car and headed inside. An intense conversation was going on in the back with some of the voices bordering on the aggressive, and Margo headed to the sun-room to snoop, but Lucy came bounding down the stairs. She put a finger on her lips signaling silence and pulled Margo upstairs.

"Miss Margo, after Miss Carolyn went downstairs, I took a peek around her room." She stepped into the quiet room and saw Ice and Fenway sprawled on the bedcovers. She was about to shoo them off, but Lucy told her the old lady didn't mind.

"So what did you find?"

"I was looking at these pictures on the mantel. Some of them are pretty old. This one is from India, I guess. That's her, Miss Carolyn, really young. The older man sitting on the bamboo chair surrounded by the standing womenfolk must be her dad. She sort of looks like him."

"Yes, you're right. And the woman with her hands on the chair must be the mom. But what am I looking at?" Margo looked and looked but didn't see anything out of the ordinary.

"Look at her, at Miss Carolyn. She looks sort of ill and bloated. Look at her dress. It looks like she was pregnant."

"Really? Let me see." Margo took the picture out of Lucy's hands and walked over to the window, where the sepia photograph would provide more details in the sunlight. "I guess you could be right. She does have a suspicious bulge under her dress. You think she could have been pregnant?"

"Look at this one. Taken at the same time, but she's standing more to one side. I say she was pregnant."

"You could be right. That would explain her sudden departure to the U.S. Isn't that what girls used to do when they got pregnant out of wedlock? Disappear, so as to not embarrass the family?"

"So you see, Miss Margo, she could have come back to Louisiana and had the baby, and then given it up for adoption. She keeps saying that she never had any children of her own. What if one of the people around her is secretly her lost child? They came back into her life looking for revenge for having been abandoned, and now they could be trying to off her and get their inheritance."

"But why bother killing her? She's old already. She's going to die any minute."

"Because they're afraid she's changing her will and cutting them out?"

"That means it has to be one of the people who already stand to inherit under the current will."

"Exactly."

"What a spider web this case is! Who all's in the sun-room?"

"Well, I think Dr. Schroeder and his wife, and the niece and the grandson with spouses."

Agnes Makóczy

"Why don't we check out the attic while everyone's busy?"

"Sounds good. Come on guys," she told Ice and Fenway as she shook them awake. "Time to work."

Chapter 24

The Attic

THE STAIRS TO THE ATTIC were at the end of the hallway of the second floor. A narrow, unfinished stairwell went on forever as it wound around and around to the topmost of the old plantation home, high up where—if you were to look out the narrow dusty windows—you would be able to see the whole city for miles around.

Margo hated attics. It was during an attic fire that she had found the murdered body of Jenny, her friend and original mother to the cats. On that same night, the old family butler, Mr. Snail and the friendly Jamaican cook Rosa Nesta had also died at the hands of a charming lunatic. Attics had nothing but miserably sad memories for her. Plus, they are always creepy, and this one was no exception. Seamstress dummies, broken mirrors, and old chairs with three legs, aren't even the worst of it. Attics are the favorite hangouts of rats and bats, and in the south, even of raccoons who find it more comfortable to live in an attic than in holes in trees under the naked stars.

Then there are the cockroaches and the spider webs. The roaches of the south are usually fat and enormous, and you can hear them rustling their wings as they slither around the room in the dark. Roaches also like to crawl into people's mouths and clean out their teeth while they sleep, or walk all over their face, sniffing their eyelids and their nose holes. Roaches tend to be an abomination. Spider webs might not be so disgusting, but many people hate them because of their poison or because their bites can cause flesh-eating disease, or simply because their webs are so gross. And then they have all those legs. The thought of getting entangled in a giant spider web nearly nauseated Margo.

So, therefore, there was nothing exciting about exploring the attic. But everyone was busy somewhere else, and Margo and Lucy had a job to do. Lucy turned the knob and peeked inside. She turned around and nodded to Margo, and the two girls stepped inside followed by Ice and Fenway.

There wasn't much light coming in from the narrow windows. The place was enormous. It encompassed the whole perimeter of the house, as if it had been a third floor, but unfinished. Shadows and dark corners mingled with broken furniture, baby cribs, armoires and chests. There were piles of bookshelves weighted down by photo albums and hardcover books. Unwanted paintings were stacked against each other by standing lamps and table lamps. Lucy flicked a light switch by the door, and the whole floor came to life. Stuffed dogs, and deer, and small bears, all smiled down dustily from the walls. One stand of shelves sported a dozen or so of wooden duck decoys, beautifully painted.

"We have to divide up," Margo told Lucy. "There's too much stuff. Do the armoires and the chests. You might find some maternity clothes."

"Would she have come to this house to have the baby?"

"Where else would she have gone? This house has been in her family for two hundred years."

Margo left Lucy rummaging through vintage clothes, which she loved to do, and she walked around raising a cloud of dust, and inspected the darker corners without any idea of what she was looking for. Ice and Fenway were crouched in a corner sniffing and scratching with a great show of enthusiasm. Ice's meow kept getting louder and more aggressive until Margo finally approached him. There was a pile of large, rolled up rugs lying on top of each other that had been pushed to the side. Fenway was sniffing at them furiously. "Lucy, come give me a hand," she said. "I think the cats found something."

They pulled the rugs to the center of the room and unrolled them one by one. They were heavy and awkward and made them sneeze. At the fourth try they both said *Oh My God* at the same time. They had just found the bloody rug.

"So this is how Sharmila cleaned the rug. By hiding it and putting another one in its place. This rug is very similar to the one downstairs, I think."

"But why would she bother?"

"I have no idea. She's a nice woman. I had a long chat with her earlier, and I just don't see her doing something like this in malice."

"Maybe she really wanted to impress Miss Carolyn because she needed the job."

"But Carolyn said that the blood kept appearing and disappearing, and that does speak of malice." Margo took a picture with her cellphone. "We have to keep going. There's a lot to go through." They moved the rugs back to where they had found them and continued their search.

After a while, Margo came across an old photo album. It was the college years of Carolyn, Dolly, Dotty and Renée. Poor Renée, how pretty she looked in the hippy era, with lots of beads and bellbottom pants and braided hair, and now she was dead. Dolly and Dotty looked like two peas in a pod even back then. Later on in the album there were pictures of babies with them in Native American child carriers called papooses. Even Carolyn had her papoose baby. The child could have belonged to one of the other friends though, but it made her wonder.

Lucy had just gone through one of the chests and walked over to where Margo was sitting on the floor by the photo albums. She handed her a pair of hand crocheted baby socks with pompons. They were yellow with age and had been washed many times. "I think she had the baby in this house," she said. "Poor Miss Carolyn. I wonder what happened to her baby."

"Yes," Margo answered her. "I wonder too. Maybe it died." Then she kept looking. In one of the albums, she stared for a good while and took out a couple of pictures from their corners. They were of a somewhat younger Dolly and a young girl with dirty-blond hair who stared at the camera with serious eyes as if she was looking through the photographer. Margo carefully placed them in a plastic baggie and put them in her shirt pocket where they wouldn't wrinkle too easily.

Chapter 25

The Sun-Room

THE GIRLS WENT STRAIGHT to the sun-room where Carolyn was presiding over her guests from her favorite rattan chair, surrounded by a pile of multicolored pillows in wild floral patterns. Sharmila was handing out pink lemonade as usual, and she smiled at Margo when she gave her a glass. Margo grinned back, happy that the hostility had vanished between them. Every time she stepped into that room, Margo was reminded of a jungle: the potted palm trees, the orchids and the other exotic plants, the fruit-laden orange trees, but especially all those windows from where you could see the backyard woods where the house had been built.

Parvati and the insignificant Matt were sitting close to Carolyn, huddled around a small card table. A young woman Margo had never seen before sat with them, making the fourth. They all had cards in their hands, and they were concentrating. Claude and Dr. Schroeder were outside, smoking. Their discussion was unpleasantly animated as usual, and Margo wished she could be a bee on a flower next to them, to hear what they were saying. The self-effacing Valeria sat quietly to one side—barely moving—staring through the window at Dr. Schroeder and her fiancé. Margo told Lucy she would be right back. Nobody seemed to notice when she stepped outside and walked over to the doctor.

Agnes Makóczy

The humidity had risen since she had gotten back, and the air was almost too heavy to breathe. She watched the two men as she walked toward them. Claude—the wonderful grandson—had an ugly smirk on his face. The more Margo saw him, the less she liked him. The patina of civility around his persona was very thin, and when it fell, it uncovered an ugly character. Nor was Dr. Schroeder a jewel. He was never a friendly man, but on this day he was in an especially foul mood. He turned around to look at Margo and wished her away with his gaze. But Margo didn't budge. She had only one question.

"Dr. Schroeder, was Renée poisoned?"

"Well, yes. According to the preliminary tests, yes she was. Something she ate, I would guess."

"Sodium Nitroprusside?" Margo expected a snide remark, but the doctor's eyes opened wide with surprise, and he stared at her.

"How did you know?"

"That's how Carolyn's dog Mutt died. Renée was given the same poison Carolyn was. But poor Mutt spilled her drink and lapped it up and died instead." Dr. Schroeder looked distraught. He muttered something under his breath and turned back toward Claude. She knew she had been dismissed.

She went back into the sun-room and sat next to Lucy.

"Who's the new girl?" she asked her.

"Didn't you know? That's Maddy. She works part time at the nursing home in Youngsville and comes here three times a week to help out. But she likes to play cards, so sometimes they call her to be the fourth. Neither Valeria nor Claude play, I've heard."

"She must be the Maddy whose phone number Ice and Fenway found in Pierre's house."

"We'll find out in a minute. Here comes Pierre." Indeed, tall, dark, and handsome, had just stepped into the sun-room and approached Carolyn and whispered something in her ear. Carolyn told him *Thank you, my dear*, and patted his hand. Then she turned back to her cards. But Maddy had been following every one of Pierre's moves as Sharmila had mentioned, with stars in her eyes. Unfortunately for the girl, he never gave her a second look. Instead, Pierre looked at her—Margo—and gave her a big warm smile. Margo realized that his smile made her blush and she fussed at herself. No playing with clients.

"Lucy, we have to go to the nursing home. I have to show Dolly and Dotty the pictures we took and ask them some questions." The two girls turned around and left the room. Nobody except for Maddy seemed to notice or to care.

Chapter 26

The Chase

MARGO HOPPED INTO THE nondescript tan car that Pierre had given her keys to, and drove away. Next to her was Lucy, riding shotgun. She was running a commentary on suburban living, making funny comments on the cows in the fields and the tractors that insisted on driving in the middle of the road slowing everyone down. She was a pleasant companion on the road: never running out of things to say. Meantime, Margo was trying to put her thoughts together, memorizing the list of questions she was going to ask Dolly and Dotty. She had only met them the once, but she was convinced they had a bucket-load of secrets concealed between the two of them, and she hoped they would be willing to share some of them.

"Miss Margo, that pickup truck behind us, it's been following us since we left the gas station," Lucy said, wondering out loud if she had been reading too many detective stories.

"Now that you mention it, it has been. Let me get to the outer lane and let him pass." Margo moved over to the slow lane to give the pickup space. She was watching it in her rearview mirror. It was enormous compared to the small car she was driving. It was threatening-looking with an indistinct patch-up of many coats of different greens. She had heard about deadly road rage incidents and was quick to be polite when necessary. But the pickup changed lanes with her and smoothly slipped in behind her. "I think you're right Lucy, he is following us," she said with a little bit of worry in her voice.

"What do we do now, Miss Margo?"

"I'm not sure," she answered, watching the pickup from the rearview mirror, thinking back to the private detective how-to manuals she had read. What do you do when you're being followed? "I'll speed up—see if it still follows us. Are you well buckled in?"

"Yes, Miss," Lucy said with her voice shaking in fear. Margo looked at her and saw that Lucy's eyes were wide open, staring mesmerized at the pickup through her side mirror.

"Hang on then, and don't be afraid. I'm a really good driver, and I'm not going to let anything bad happen to you." Margo was speaking with a self-assurance she was very far from feeling. This was a really deserted road. And she didn't know her way around. They had left most of the town behind them, and she couldn't see any place where she could stop for help. Anything she tried was pointless. Whenever Margo sped up, the pickup followed, when she slowed down, it did the same thing.

"What does it want with us?" asked Lucy, "I'm getting scared."

"I have no idea."

They had been driving for a good five minutes that felt like an hour and a half. Margo's hands were tight on the wheel at the 10pm and 2pm positions. Her knuckles were white with stress, and her heartbeats had picked up the tempo. "We'll be okay, Lucy, don't worry. Just hang on."

The road suddenly changed from a four-lane to a two-lane and the median vanished, and it was bad. The holes in the pavement—added to the refuse that had fallen off the sugar cane trucks—made the driving harder. Margo looked at the gas meter. No need to worry about that as she had tanked not long ago. She probably had enough gas to make it back home to Half Moon Bay. But the problem was that she was lost. She had no idea where she was heading. She had been supposed to go in a straight line for four miles as the bird flies and then turn right, and she would be in Youngsville close to the nursing home, but that was many miles ago. The road kept deteriorating, and she slowed down a little to avert the ditches. But to her surprise, the truck didn't. It was so close that she could almost feel the driver breathe down her neck. She ventured a quick look at Lucy—who was as white as a sheet—hanging onto the door with one hand, and her purse with the other. She seemed to be in shock.

There were no other cars on the road, just her and the pickup. Now she was getting really scared. All she could see around were fields and fields of resting soil, with the occasional cow here and there, but no gas stations, no main roads, and no place where she could take refuge.

The first time the pickup bumped her it was a surprise. Never for a second did she think it was really out to hurt them. All she felt was the smallest tap, a tentative tap. Then she kept going. Margo was terrified. Without a GPS, she had no way to know where they were heading. The driver of the pickup seemed to be steering them in a forward direction which could easily end up at a river bank, a precipice, or the Gulf of Mexico. She thought about her little Glock, and with her heart in her mouth pulled the purse closer to her and felt for it. It was there, thank God. If they ever stopped and were confronted, she would have a way to defend herself.

The next bump was horrible. There was nothing tentative about it. She felt propelled forward and then slammed backwards, and thought for a second that her neck was broken. But still she was cool headed enough to keep control of the vehicle. She hung on tight. Other than a minor slip on the sandy road, the tires had held just fine. She continued on, focusing on the road.

THE VANISHING BLOODSTAIN

Then came the next bump. And the next one. One after the other—barely giving her time to catch her breath—the pickup kept ramming into them, hitting them harder and harder, beating them forward relentlessly. She finally lost control of the little car. She hit a patch of something slippery, and they were propelled forward as if they were flying in the air. Time slowed down, and Margo saw how the car slowly skipped the lane. She saw another car coming straight at her, and somehow they missed each other, but by mere inches. Then her car continued on. She stayed in the wrong lane for a second or two, and then kept her eastward trek and slipped off the road altogether.

The bushes were thick with flowers, and Margo was shocked that she had noticed them. Time had slowed down so much that she could even see the leaves of the bushes that had been torn off by the impact slowly gliding around her like someone had grabbed a handful of them and thrown them up into the air. Then the car slammed straight into the flowery bushes, and you could hear the branches screeching and scraping against the paint, scratching grooves into the bare metal. And then the car stopped. The sudden silence slapped her awake from the hypnotic daze in which she had been stuck. Instinctively, Margo shut the ignition off and realized she never thought to hit the brakes. Maybe that had been a good thing, maybe not.

She was dizzy and disoriented. She'd never been this scared in her whole life. She put her head back against the seat rest and closed her eyes. Breathe, breathe, she told herself, trying to calm down. With eyes closed she could hear Lucy whimpering, and reached for her hand. It was shaking, and hers was too, but at least they were both alive.

After a few minutes, she heard people running toward the car. Kindly hands opened the doors and helped her and Lucy out. The car was a wreck, but it had been a good car. It had kept them alive. She heard the ambulance wailing, coming closer, and in a daze accepted to be given a quick checkup. But she was fine. She saw the paramedics stretching Lucy out on a stretcher. One of them told her Lucy was all right, but would have to go to the hospital just in case. She ran to the ambulance and barely had time to give Lucy a hug and tell her she loved her before they took off. She was relieved to see Lucy smiling back at her. It would all be fine. Then, on shaking legs, she went back to thank the people who had come to their help: a sweet older couple with a ton of grinning teenagers. They had been the ones in the car she almost hit as she changed lanes. The parents looked startled as if still in shock, but the kids had thought it had all been an awesome adventure and were running around, taking numerous pictures with their cellphones. She cried as she hugged them and thanked them. But she was not crying for herself. She was crying for Lucy who had been hurt because of her. She would have never been able to forgive herself if something had happened to that sweet, kind soul.

Chapter 27
The Fire Next Door

ONE HOUR LATER MARGO was standing in front of Number 2 Old Plantation Road, waiting patiently for Benoît to come to the door. She waved a thank you to the State Police for dropping her off and stepped shakily into the house. It was nice and dark in the foyer. She had a longing for an armchair in a quiet spot to give her throbbing head a momentary reprieve. But she didn't get a chance. The first thing she heard was loud bickering coming from the back of the house and naturally started heading that way. Benoît looked at her with big inquisitive eyes—startled at her disheveled appearance—and discreetly offered an arm which she accepted gratefully. She had never been in this much pain as long as she had lived. Her body was painfully sore, and her head had been tossed back and forth like an ice cube in a blender.

The argument out back was escalating. Carolyn was trying to calm things down, but her voice kept getting shouted down, and the argument just got louder. But Benoît, like a good butler, wasn't easy to ruffle. He continued his steady, reliable, dignified shuffle toward the back of the house, holding up Margo's shaking body the best he could with his slender frame.

They stepped together into the sun-room, and Benoît announced her in his magnificent melodious voice as if she was the Queen of Something and not road kill. Everybody stopped yelling and turned around, surprised. Eyes popped open and mouths went agape when they saw what was left of Margo.

For one thing, Margo was barefoot. She had been wearing pumps earlier in the day. One of the heels had broken off after the accident, and it was impossible to walk in them, so she tossed them. Her skirt was torn. Her white shirt had come out from under the waist of the skirt, and a couple of the buttons were missing, showing too much cleavage. Her dainty lace cardigan was shredded, with threads hanging. There were flowers and leaves stuck in her hair and scrapes on her face and neck. And there was quite a lot of dirt on her hands and her face as well. She had survived the accident fine, but by the time she had climbed out of the ravine with the help of the good Samaritans, the shrubbery had reduced her to this mess.

She looked around suspiciously. One of these horrible people had done this to her and Lucy. She wanted to scream at them. They thought she would never discover who it was. Well, they were wrong!

There was the good doctor sitting close to the window, ill at ease. Valeria, Claude, Parvati, Matt, and Pierre had been arguing. They were all frozen in aggressive postures, staring at her angrily. Carolyn was just then trying to struggle her aging plump body up out of the chair with the help of Sharmila. Behind Sharmila stood Maddy, Pierre's Maddy. Her face was an inscrutable mask of stone where not a muscle twitched. She stared at Margo with cold eyes.

She gave everyone a quick update on what had happened while she watched them all carefully. She mentally took note of who twitched with discomfort, and whose eyes had an extra guilty glint. The guests watched each other just as carefully, surreptitiously, curiously wondering—she presumed—which one of them in that room had tried to kill her, or at least scare her away from reaching the nursing home. Then she told them she was going to go talk to Brooks and left them standing there. Not a word had been said. But when she stepped out, she heard the conversation resume as if someone had put the needle back on the LP record.

She left through the back door wondering what they were talking about behind her back. She borrowed a pair of yard clogs from the mud room that were too big on her, and she clopped on the walkway carefully—knees shaking—still not recovered from the shock she had just been through.

It was soothing to walk in the hushed quiet of the backyard. It was good to be alive, too. The cool air refreshed her and revived her. She walked on the moist blanket of leaves underfoot noticing as she went that the salmon pink azaleas and the wine red ones had opened already. She was going to tell Brooks that they needed to plant more azaleas. Someone had made an effort at picking up the branches from the ground and had put them in scattered piles around the backyard. The last rays of the setting sun filtered through the thick foliage overhead, but provided no warmth. Margo was starting to feel the after-effects of the accident. She was shivering with cold.

There were birds chirping. The sounds from the busy street were muted by the heavy foliage but once in a while you could still hear a police siren or an ambulance zoom by. Before she knocked on the door, she gathered her composure and smoothed her clothes down. Lucy and Brooks were very fond of each other, and he was going to be very upset when he heard the news.

Once inside, Margo sat down and listened to Brooks rant and rave for a while, and when he calmed down some, she told him to pack.

"I think that it's best for you two to take the Mercedes and go back home in the morning. I already pretty much know what's going on, and after I turn in my report, I'll either get a ride from someone or rent a car. I want Lucy at home resting and out of the way. And you might as well take the cats. I want you all safely out of the way." Brooks just paced up and down in the small parlor, nodding his head.

"I'll go pick up Lucy at the hospital, and after a good night's rest, she'll be ready to hit the road again," he added, still nodding from time to time. "But I hate to leave you alone. Are you sure you can manage on your own?"

"I'll be fine."

Brooks and Margo stood at the front of the guest house and discussed some of the finer points of the case. Before they knew it, it had become dark. There, beneath the extensive canopy of leaves, darkness came early. They were slowly heading toward the house when Brooks nudged Margo.

"It smells funny. Look, something's burning. Can you see the fire?"

"It's coming from next door. Let's go check it out," Margo said, heading in that direction. "It's the neighbors. They're probably going to barbecue."

They approached the flimsy chicken-wire fence separating the two houses cautiously. People were arguing. Margo looked at Brooks and put her index finger on her lips. They got as close as they dared and positioned themselves behind some azaleas.

Sanders and Laura Lane's backyard was a big clearing in the forest of oak trees. They had a nice looking tennis court and a patio with chairs, a table, and umbrella. An oil drum had been set up on one side of the patio, and flames were shooting out of it burning blue and yellow and orange. Sanders Lane was fanning the flames.

"Hurry up, Laura," they heard him yell toward the house. "The fire's going to die out."

Brooks and Margo turned their heads to the back door in unison and saw Laura coming out with an armful of papers. Sanders helped her toss them in the fire. Then they heard someone approaching from the road and turned that way to look.

THE VANISHING BLOODSTAIN

"I know what you're doing, and it's not going to work," a familiar voice called out to them with contempt in his voice as he walked toward the couple in the backyard. "It's no use burning them. I have copies, and you know it."

"You bastard, leave us alone already." Sanders faced the oil drum again and threw some more papers into the fire. There was a feverish, maniacal look in his eyes. Burning sparks poured out of the oil drum, and the breeze blew the embers away into the wind, illuminating for brief seconds the night like tiny ephemeral fireflies. Sanders kept fanning the fire. "You're not getting another penny."

The familiar voice just laughed. "Look who's here. You have company," the voice said in a mocking tone, and Sanders and Laura both looked toward the driveway. The newcomers had arrived separately. The driveway was dark, and all Brooks and Margo could distinguish in the penumbra were the illuminated faces of Sanders and Laura, standing by the burning oil drum, both looking like they wanted to run away. They took a few steps and joined the others in the driveway, and Brooks and Margo couldn't see them anymore. They waited for a while, but it seemed like the Lanes and their guests had moved into the house. "Never mind," Margo told Brooks, "I know who they are, and I know what's going on. Let's go back."

So Brooks went to visit Lucy at the hospital and tell her that they were leaving in the morning, and Margo went upstairs to get a shower before dinner time. Then, she suddenly remembered the cats. They hadn't been at Brooks', and they hadn't been in the sun-room. If they had been downstairs, they would have come looking for her. They always did.

She went into Lucy's room at the top of the stairs, but no Ice and Fenway. She was starting to worry now. She peeked into Carolyn's room and nothing. If they weren't downstairs, and they weren't upstairs, where could they be? She started calling them. She walked around the upstairs, calling their names, opening bedroom doors and closet doors. She listened for Ice's meow. Fenway cried so softly that she would never be able to hear her, but Ice had a loud and bossy voice. She closed her eyes and listened. She thought she heard noises upstairs and just to be for sure, she climbed the winding stairs to the attic. She stared horrified at the attic door. Lucy and her had somehow closed the door behind them and left the cats behind. But no, no way. She distinctly remembered leaving the door open and propping it up with a pile of heavy books. She always did. There was no way she would have left her babies behind, trapped like that. Someone must have closed it after they left.

Horror scenarios danced grotesquely in front of her eyes. *We could have died on that road to nowhere today, and Ice and Fenway would have been left trapped in the attic to die of thirst and hunger.* She lunged for the door and yanked it open, expecting a volley of disapproval and anger coming from the cats. They could be very verbose when they were displeased. But no sound came from the door, and no cats came bounding out like chased by a fox. Intrigued, she turned the light on and was shocked to realize that she hadn't been missed at all. Fenway was sleeping pleasantly sprawled on an old armchair and barely lifted her head to acknowledge Margo's presence. Ice was sitting on a pile of yellowed newspapers in a corner by the rugs.

Margo ran to them with an aching heart, regretting miserably having forgotten all about them. She picked up little Fenway and gave her a ton of kisses, and then ran to Ice. But he didn't want to be picked up. He clung with his nails to the jute string that was tying the old newspapers. Margo bent down curiously to look at them. The photograph of someone she had seen before stared at her from the paper on the front page. It had been breaking news. She looked through the other papers and had to laugh out loud. She had just cracked the case.

Chapter 28

The Crew Goes Home

SHE HAD JUST CRACKED THE CASE. Or so she thought. Lucy and Brooks left early the next morning taking the cats with them. Not two hours later, Carolyn got a devastating phone call that just about killed her. Her beloved grandson Claude had been found on the golf course by an employee of the Country Club. He died in the arms of the said employee in great pain. That was all the family knew.

Pierre drove Margo to the club as fast as he dared, zooming recklessly through narrow streets. Sharmila was looking after Carolyn, and her doctor was on the way. But Margo had to get to the club before every inch of the place was trampled down again. Walking through the foyer, she wished she had a badge to show the people so they would move out of her way. Pierre took long steps trying to keep up with her. She was in a tear.

The employee who had found Claude, Ernesto, was a young kid with zits that had probably just gotten his worker's permit. He was flustered with excitement, the way only teenage boys can when faced with the ugly gore of life and death situations. She followed the young man briskly to where he had found Claude by the golf course—lying on the wet grass—twisted into a fetal position by the pain. His clothes were moist, Ernesto said, so he could have lain there for hours before the sprinklers came on.

Agnes Makóczy

Pierre and Ernesto stood quietly to the side while Margo walked the perimeter trying to spot something out of place that the police might have missed. She knew Claude. He must have had a rendezvous to meet someone, or else he wouldn't have bothered coming all the way out here. The club was at the outskirts of town, and once night fell and the guests went home, it would be as dead as a cemetery. No. Claude came out here to meet someone. He would have smoked while he stood there waiting, like he had done in front of Carolyn's house. He could never go for more than a few minutes without lighting one up.

The grass was all trampled again, all the way down to the mud. She concentrated on the bushes. Claude was fond of tossing his cigarette stubs under the bushes. After a few long minutes of search and squat, search and squat, she found a cigarette stub under a dwarf dogwood that fit the bill. She touched the mulch under the bush and found it to be dry. Because the sprinklers hadn't reached all the way here, the cigarette stub had been preserved dry. It wasn't the same brand that Claude usually smoked, but she could bet her whole inheritance that it would have his DNA on the filter. She picked it up carefully with a plastic baggie and placed it in a small box in her purse. This was one piece of evidence she was going to have to take good care of.

She walked back to where Pierre and the boy were standing.

"Ernesto," she said, pulling the boy to the side so Pierre couldn't hear them. "You say the man was still alive when you found him, right?"

"Yes, ma'am, he was alive, and he was crying. I think he was in a lot of pain." Ernesto was standing up straight, aware of his importance as a witness. He slipped his hand into his uniform pocket and brought out a piece of notebook paper. He handed it to Margo.

"What's this, Ernesto?" she asked, staring at the words scribbled on it.

"That's what he said, ma'am. I wrote it down so I wouldn't forget." Ernesto looked like he was mighty proud of himself.

"He told you this before he died? Are you sure this is what he said?"

"Yes, ma'am. He said it twice. Then he started crying again. He was holding his stomach like he was in a lot of pain. He said, 'Tell her. She needs to know.' He made me promise I would tell. And then he died."

Margo looked at the young man with a newfound respect. "You're a very clever young man. It was a great idea to write it down." She gave him a big smile so he could see how pleased she was. She remembered well what it was like to be young and awkward and underappreciated. "But how come you didn't give this to the police?" she asked.

An astute glint shone in Ernesto's eyes. "They were rude to me. And none of them were women. The dying man said 'tell her' and so I waited for a woman to come and question me. A woman who looked smart enough to understand what he was talking about."

"You amaze me, young Ernesto. I have a feeling that you'll go far in life. Thank you very much. Thank you very much indeed." She shook the young man's hand gratefully and went to look for Pierre. She couldn't have been happier if she had won the lottery. This time the case was really solved.

Chapter 29

Carolyn's Story

MARGO FOUND CAROLYN upstairs sitting all alone, by the window in her bedroom. The lights hadn't been turned on. A meager light was filtering through the heavy branches adding a touch of sadness to the quiet room. She hadn't wanted to go downstairs. She looked devastated. Her eyes were swollen with tears, and there was a greenish pallor to her skin. Margo approached her slowly and pulled up a chair. She grabbed one of Carolyn's shaking hands and patted it.

"I'm sorry you've had to go through so much. And we're not done yet. I have to tell you something that might or might not make you happy. I found your baby."

"What do you mean, you found my baby?"

"Well, the first time I met your friends, you told the story of your childhood in India, and how you had moved here to go to college, remember? Digging up old records, I found out that you came back here to have a baby."

Margo had underestimated the effect that the news would have on Carolyn. She got up painstakingly and faced Margo, leaning on her walking stick. She looked bewildered as if someone had slapped her. Her whole body was shaking.

"Please don't, Margo. I can't bear to talk about this," she said. The tears had started running down her face again. She lifted a hand as if she were trying to push the news away. "I've had to live with this all my life, and it has torn me into pieces. Please let's talk of something else." Her rheumy eyes were rimmed with red and pleaded silently with Margo.

"Please don't hate me. I know this is very private, but I had to explore the possibility that your own descendants found out who you were and are now trying to kill you to get their inheritance."

"It makes no sense, Margo. If that's what they're after, why kill Claude?"

"Because he was going to get the bulk of your estate. With him out of the way, there's more to inherit."

"And you say you found my baby?"

"Yes. Don't worry, Miss Carolyn. Father Armand didn't tell me your secret. It happened by a series of accidents. You had a daughter that you named Margaret. You had her with you for a while but later gave her up for adoption, right?"

"It wasn't because I didn't love her. It was because I wanted her to have a real family and a normal life. She was in danger, and I had to keep her safe. I found her a good home. I did what was best for her, but it broke my heart." Carolyn started crying again. Her little handkerchief was completely soaked, and Margo rummaged in the drawers until she found her a clean one. She helped Carolyn sit back down.

"This house is haunted. No, don't look at me like that, Margo. It really is. When I was a little girl, my older sister Lizzie and I used to be terrified of leaving our room at night. Several times we saw ghosts walking downstairs when everyone was sleeping. One night, we decided to go downstairs and see for ourselves. Lizzie was scared, but I kept begging, so we went. Last minute, I got frightened and ran back upstairs, but Lizzie continued on. Suddenly, there was a terrible commotion. Something broke, and Lizzie screamed, and my parents woke up and ran downstairs, and we looked for my sister but she had vanished."

"Oh my God, what do you mean she had vanished?"

"She had been kidnapped. Father hoped she had wandered outside, and he and the servants and the dogs looked everywhere, but she was gone."

"Did they ever find her?"

"Actually, yes. A few days later the police brought her back home. She was wet, and cold, and crying. They found her out in the fields somewhere around New Iberia. She wasn't hurt, just terrified. She said she couldn't remember much. Someone covered her head with a sack and drove her to an empty shack and left her there. There was food and water, so she was okay for a day or so, but then she got scared that the people were going to come back and started looking for a way to escape. She managed to pry the bug screen off of the bathroom window. It was very small and high up, but it had no bars. She propped a little table under it and then a chair on top of that, and squeezed and squeezed her body through until she was free."

"So she escaped, and the police brought her home?"

"Yes. She told the police she didn't remember anything, but she told Father more than that."

"Do you know what?"

"No. He and Mother never talked about it again. But then, the messages started appearing on the wall by the front door. They looked like they had been painted in blood, at least that's what the servants said. They were terrifying. One was *your child will die* and there was another one that I was very scared of: *I swear to you that I will kill her.* The servants white-washed them, but after a few days they would appear again. Mother and Father were very frightened. Then, one day, Father said at breakfast time that we were leaving. He had had enough. We were going back to India."

"I'm confused. So you were born in India but you spent a few years here in Lafayette before going back?"

"Sorry, my dear. I'm rambling. Let me start at the beginning. It all began when my mother traveled to India to meet my father. My sister was born, and a few years later I came along. Father had a secret. He had killed an important man in an unlawful duel, and he couldn't go back to England, or else, he risked being hanged. But in India nobody cared. He never said, but he was sort of hiding out there. But Mother wasn't happy. The insalubrious climate was tough on her health, so Father decided to come to Louisiana where Mother's family had a plantation, and give life here a try.

"So we moved into this house, and we were very happy for a while. Then Lizzie and I started seeing ghosts. Of course, nobody believed us. So Lizzie went downstairs one night to investigate, and that's when the kidnapping happened. Father was terrified. He packed the household up, and we set off for New Orleans. From there on, we were going to board a ship and head for India. We packed up the cars and the luggage, and a number of servants were coming with us as well.

"There was a lot of confusion, I remember. Even the dogs were coming. Mother had refused to leave them behind. Just imagine the commotion. We settled for the trip, and by the time we got to New Orleans, Lizzie was nowhere to be found. Somehow in the confusion she disappeared. We never saw her again. Father left us in New Orleans and went back to look for her. He was gone for weeks, but when he came to get us there was no Lizzie. We never did hear from her again.

"Mother got sick from the anguish and refused to eat or sleep. All she did was cry for her baby. But we kept on going. Father was afraid of putting my life and Mother's life in danger. So we went to India and disappeared."

"And you never found out what happened to Lizzie?"

Agnes Makóczy

"No. Never."

"Carolyn, why are you telling me all this? It's all so private."

"Because maybe you can help me."

"I don't see how I could help. It all happened so long ago."

"Well, let me finish telling you. Mother eventually got used to her life there. She was always sad when it was Lizzie'z birthday, or Christmas, but she got on well enough. Then one day I got pregnant. You have to understand that back then in India, this was not the end of the world. The British made their own laws and lived by their own rules. Father was an important plantation owner and cared very little about the opinions of others, and he loved me enough to not judge me. But my baby's father was also an important man, an Indian landowner. He wanted to marry me and take over the care of my child. He saw in it a political alliance. He wanted me to remain in India forever. Going to college was out of question. I would be locked up in a house together with my mother-in-law and her husband, and that was a fate worse than death. I had been raised free as a bird. I would have killed myself before moving in with that nasty woman that was his mother. I knew well what women like her did to their little daughters-in-law."

"So you escaped?"

"Yes. Father and Mother smuggled me out of there, and I was on the first boat headed to Louisiana. I came back to Lafayette and moved into the old homestead. I had my baby here and was very happy for a while. I started going to the same university Pierre goes to now, except that then it was called the University of Southwestern Louisiana, and I studied Liberal Arts. That's where I became friends with Dolly, Dotty and Renée. We were all young mothers going to school, and of course we bonded.

"I had a wonderful ayah, a young Cajun girl who had recently lost her children to influenza. She became Margaret's second mother. Then the messages started appearing again, but this time in the baby's room, right over her crib. *Your baby will die* was the scariest, but there were a number of them. We washed them off and painted them over, but after a few days a new message would appear, painted in what looked like blood. I can't begin to tell you how horrified I was. It was like a curse that was following me through my life wherever I went."

"But Carolyn, did you consider that someone in your household was painting them on the wall?"

"No, I didn't. I was too terrified. Besides, who would do such a cruel thing?" Carolyn had stopped crying and was now sitting up straight, looking at Margo with interest.

"For example, the same people that painted on the walls when you were little. The modus operandi is too similar."

"I know, but this was twenty years later."

"There might be a connection."

"Anyway, it was in those days that we had that accursed party. I was in no mood, but the girls wouldn't let it go. I had been too scared to tell them about the threats on the nursery wall, and they didn't know how depressed and scared I was. I finally relented, and the house filled with guests, and there was too much drinking and merrymaking. Suddenly I remember people screaming, and a dead body on the floor. Everyone vanished as if the house had caught on fire. I ran upstairs to check on the baby."

"You told the police you didn't remember anything."

"Of course I did. I was trying to be inconspicuous, to not call attention to myself. That same night I decided to give my baby away. The ayah and her husband were thrilled. They truly loved Margaret. I gave them enough money to buy a good house and enough money for a lifetime, and I never saw them again. Then I closed down the house, packed my bags and left."

"What happened with your friends?"

"I told them the baby had died, and I was heartbroken and was going away for a while. I asked them not to ever mention her name again, and they never did. And I was really heartbroken. So I went to England and stayed with cousins and never came back until much later when I was already married to John."

"Carolyn, that's a very sad story, but I still don't understand why you're telling me all this."

"Because the story is not over." Carolyn bent her head down on her chest and started crying softly again. Margo waited patiently. After a few minutes she stopped sobbing and told the rest of her story.

"Back when I lived here with my baby, servants used to say that there were ghosts walking around at night. But it's a big house. It creaks and groans when the weather changes, and it's easy to imagine things going bump in the night. But they insisted it was ghosts. White, translucent, quiet ghosts that would appear in one corner, walk a few feet, and then vanish at the next corner. It was like when Lizzy and I were little. I was terrified but tried not to show it. I kept telling them that they were imagining things."

"Oh my God," Margo burst out and looked at the distraught old woman. "You've seen them again."

"Yes. Ever since Mutt died. They come out at night when I go upstairs to sleep. I know it when they come. I can hear them. A few times I turned around as I walked upstairs, and I saw the miasma spreading, covering the floor around the stairs, silent and ghostly like the fog, and I'm too scared to go down and check it out. Oh, Margo, what am I going to do?" Carolyn started crying again. She leaned over to Margo and put her head on her shoulder. Margo patted her back gently trying to figure out what on earth she was going to do.

"Don't despair, Carolyn," she said finally after a few minutes. "I just had an idea. I'm convinced this is a flesh and blood creature you're talking about and not a ghostly one. I'll prove it to you. We'll set a trap during Renée's wake."

Chapter 30
Pierre, Benoît, And The Plan

MARGO RAN DOWN THE STAIRS with renewed enthusiasm. With some luck she would be able to close a new case, and an old one, and give this poor woman some peace of mind. She ran into Sharmila, who almost dropped the tea she was about to carry upstairs for Carolyn.

"Don't go anywhere, Sharmila. I need to talk to you in Carolyn's room. I'll be back in ten minutes."

Then, Margo went to fetch Pierre and Benoît to ask for help. Because men don't like it so much when the good ideas come from women, they huffed and puffed a little, but Margo could be as bossy as anyone when she had to be, and finally they agreed to help her. The finer points were up to them, and she didn't care how they achieved them, as long as they agreed on the rest.

Chapter 31

Sharmila's Story

SHARMILA HAD A GOOD IDEA of what was coming. She imagined—as if in a nightmare—being dismissed from her job and sent back to Deorala in disgrace. Because, where else would she go? Carolyn was her only family except for distant relatives in India who despised her. She heard Margo's footsteps creaking on the stairs, coming closer and closer, and she braced herself. Margo pulled up a chair in front of Carolyn and told Sharmila to come and sit.

"Carolyn" Margo told the old woman, "Sharmila has something to tell you about the bloody rug and the things around the house that move from place to place when you're not looking. I have a feeling that she had strong reasons to do what she did, so hear her out first before you judge."

Sharmila pointedly looked at her sandaled feet and the hem of her salwar kameez, and wished she was many, many miles away. She wished Margo would stop talking.

"I asked Sharmila the other day where she was from, and she said Deorala," Margo continued. "That's in India. There was a famous case of lynching and riots in Deorala a few years back, and I looked it up. A woman named Jaswinder almost became the victim of that lynching, and I remember Sharmila mentioned once that her mother's name was also Jaswinder. The scandal was big enough that it made it to the newspapers, and now it's on the internet. I also found out that Parvati's family must have given her refuge or helped her in some way, because her family was living close to Deorala at the time of the lynching. There had to be a connection. The coincidence was too great."

Sharmila looked sideways at Carolyn who had a puzzled look on her face. Obviously she had no idea what the other two were talking about. Sharmila knew that the moment of truth had come. And there was nowhere to run. She needed to unburden her heart anyway. This had been such a degrading experience that she could no longer keep it inside.

Sharmila swallowed hard and looked around. Everyone was listening. "Yes, that was Jaswinder, my mom. It happened when I was a baby," she began quietly. "It was the year 1960. My mother was very young. More often than not, marriages in India are arranged. But she had married for love a young man who worked for Parvati's family. We were living in the district of Sikar in Rajasthan, in Deorala Village. My mother was very happy. She had a newborn baby, me. But soon after I was born there was a horrible hunting accident, and my father was killed along with some other workers and members of Parvati's family.

"Jaswinder realized her life was over. Widowhood is a state of social death in India, even among the higher castes. For women left behind by their husbands, it's better to be dead. Therefore, it's customary for a wife to commit *suttee* if her husband has died. That's suicide by fire. They make a funeral pyre to burn the body of the husband, and the widow will jump on the fire and be burned alive with him, sometimes even carrying her young children with her to their death.

"It's not always a voluntary death. If the crowd becomes intoxicated with alcohol and bloodlust, and the widow tries to change her mind about jumping in the pyre, they will gladly throw her into the fire themselves. It's hard to believe that suttee still exists in the 21st century, but even today, it is more common than the authorities would like you to believe. It has been banned and outlawed over and over again, but the people don't care. Their lust for blood and sacrifice is too great to allow the custom to die. And they will travel long distances to witness such a spectacle.

"So, they erected a funeral pyre for my father in the town center. He was draped in a white shroud and placed on a huge pile of wood. They lighted the fire, and he started to burn. There were hundreds of spectators gathered already, but more were arriving by the minute. Word had spread that there would be a suttee in Deorala, and people were coming from far and away to enjoy it.

"Jaswinder—my mother—stood a few feet away, holding me in her arms. The stench of burning flesh and the black smoke that rose from the funeral pyre made my mother cry. But she was also crying because the fate of a widow in India is very dire, and she foresaw a miserable future for us. Not only had she lost her beloved young husband, but she would now probably face having to beg to sustain us both. We would be degraded and shunned.

"Even with those horrors facing her, my mother told me she never intended to jump in the fire. She loved me dearly and wanted me to have a chance at life, but the crowd was cheering, egging her on. They wanted blood. A mutiny was spreading through the crowd. They were getting loud and angry. They wanted Jaswinder to jump in. When she saw what was going on, she started taking steps backward, looking for a way to escape. The crowd was fast becoming a lynch mob.

"When her sister-in-law Padma saw that my mother was trying to escape, she jumped out from the crowd and started pulling her toward the fire, hurling insulting words at her. If you don't jump in the fire voluntarily, they call you whore, and husband eater, and other ugly things. When they saw Padma pulling us toward the fire, the crowd got excited. They would get their spectacle after all. She pulled hard and Jaswinder resisted, but little by little she was losing ground and getting ever closer to the fire. She could already feel the heat from the flames of the pyre burning her skin and the heavy smoke in her eyes and her throat, and I started to cry. The crowd was getting drunk with alcohol and bloodlust. Jaswinder kept getting pulled closer and closer to the funeral pyre. It seemed that we were going to die for sure.

"Then, out of the horizon, like an angel of salvation, Parvati's father—together with a dozen or so Englishmen—rode into the town square on their horses. Armed to the teeth and shooting into the air, they pushed the crowd away from where Jaswinder was standing holding me, and beat them back with swords and clubs. Shots were fired and some people fell wounded.

"The confusion gave Parvati's father enough time to pick my mother and me up and throw us on the back of his horse. In the meantime, the Englishmen covered his back, and when Jaswinder and I were safely on the back of his horse, they rode out of town as swiftly as they had arrived. It was a miracle. It could have all gone so wrong, but somehow it worked.

"This is how her father saved us. I grew up in their household, and my mother lived to a fairly old age. They gave me an education and a good life, and they stood by me. The town folks always despised me because they knew about the failed suttee, but I never felt like an outcast at home because Parvati's family cared for me. I have always owed an enormous debt of gratitude to them for this, and will until the day I die."

Sharmila looked at Carolyn and saw the horror and the pity on her face. "So when Parvati asked me to help her drive you crazy, I was honor-bound to do it, but I love you, Shrimati, like I would love a mother and it killed me inside to hurt you. What choice did I have?" Large tears were running down Sharmila's face and she looked pleadingly at Carolyn, her eyes big and sad. "I came to Lafayette to find a job in your home as she instructed me to. Then, I did everything she told me."

Carolyn struggled out of her chair and finally managed to get up. Sharmila had extended a hand to help her, but Carolyn gently pushed it away—but without unkindness—and walked slowly to the window. Out there, far away, the day was pretty. It was cheerful and sunny. But here in this darkened room full of tear stained faces, there was nothing sunny about life.

"Margo," she said. "Tell me this at least. Is Parvati really my niece?"

"Yes, she is. My police friends in Half Moon Bay found out that she's indeed your sister's daughter. I'm sorry."

"My little sister was always a horrid creature. I didn't see her many times, but I never missed her. Parvati probably takes after her mother. I'm not sure I'll ever be able to forgive her."

"Shrimati," the distraught maid said, "I'll pack up my things and leave in the morning. I don't expect you to forgive me. I'll never forgive myself."

"Don't be silly, my dear," Carolyn told her with a shaky voice. "At least I know I'm not going senile. And I understand you well. I lived enough years in India to understand being honor-bound. You had no choice. Now go and get us some fresh tea. I need to talk to Margo in private."

Chapter 32

The Wake

A LONG LINE OF CARS STARTED ARRIVING in front of the house on Old Plantation Road. It had been raining all day, and the guests entered the house sad, wet, and grumpy. Pierre, Sharmila, and Benoît, helped unburden them of raincoats and umbrellas, and showed them the way to the living room which was darker and gloomier and much more appropriate for the occasion than the riotously cheerful sun-room.

Renée had acquired many friends and acquaintances during her long life. Members of the nursing home—too infirm to come on their own—had been chauffeured over, and there were a number of people from church who Carolyn recognized and pointed out. Soon there was barely any room to move in the house.

"Carolyn," Margo asked, "where is Renée's family? You did say she had children and grandchildren, didn't you?"

"Well, yes. She had one daughter that I know of, and I remember her mentioning her grandchildren, but I haven't seen them in years. I don't even remember what they look like. We just never talked about them. Are you still worried that one of them might be here waiting for another opportunity to get rid of me?"

"It could very well be. Just remember please to not eat or drink anything unless Sharmila gives it to you personally."

"I know, I know."

"I'll mingle. See if I can find anything out. Benoît is ready."

"Let's wait until everyone's settled down."

"Okay."

The nursing home staff and the chauffeurs were being served food and drinks back in the expansive kitchens. The only one there with the guests was Renée's chauffeur, and it surprised Margo that he should have been fond enough of the old woman to even bother coming to her wake. She wondered how many people would attend Claude's wake, once his body had been released by the police. He was probably nowhere nearly as well loved as Renée had been.

The connecting French doors between the living room and the dining room had been opened, and a catered spread had been set out on the large dining room table. Wine-spiced tea was served from a large silver Russian samovar on a sideboard—in the good china. Extra chairs had been rented to accommodate all the guests.

Margo walked around discreetly, listening to snippets of conversation. They were mostly about the deceased. She hadn't led a particularly interesting life nor had had any kind of distinguishing career, but people sounded fond of her. Renée had been sort of a nice person, apparently liked by all. It was a shame that she had to die such a horrible death. Baffling, really, that anyone should have felt the need to kill her. And yet, someone had. Unless she was mistaken, and the poison had really been intended for Carolyn, and Renée got stuck with it by mistake.

Parvati and Valeria were both dressed in black. Black made Parvati look frumpy, and Valeria, sallow. It was a color that suited neither of them. She was pleased that Matt had shoes on that hid his disgusting feet. They were standing next to the drapes by one of the cathedral windows, whispering of course. She approached them to say hello, and they all greeted her with their usual hostile glances. She wondered what Valeria was doing there. After all, with Claude dead, her presence had become unnecessary.

Sanders and Laura Lane were finally dressed appropriately. A former senator surely couldn't appear in front of all these rich people looking like a slob. They were standing in a corner next to Alfred Bailey, who was forced to drink tea because alcohol wasn't being served at the wake. Poor Lila sure had her hands full. But she obviously loved him. Maybe one day Alfred would learn to measure up to his full potential. Lila sat with some very well dressed middle-aged folks from church. She was impeccably dressed, making everyone else around her look drab. Lila looked up and gave Margo a big smile and waved. It was impossible not to like Lila.

She looked around for Dr. Schroeder and found him and Bernice sitting on a couch by the nursing home crowd. He looked so haggard that he could easily have been mistaken for one of them. Bernice had on one of her inappropriate tights, but she looked more conservative than usual. It was obvious she was trying. Poor Bernice. It seemed that nobody liked her. She approached the group and said hello. Bernice looked at her, and Margo gave her a friendly smile. Bernice smiled back gratefully. She looked so lost.

By and by, they all settled down with their platefuls of comfort food. The rain was pouring by the bucket-load, beating harshly on the cathedral windows in the living room. Even at its best, the chandelier above their heads provided an insufficient light, and the room remained gloomy and darkish. The stormy weather was so loud that it dampened people's willingness to chitchat, and they soon sat back and stopped trying. As the hush descended on the company, Benoît—the butler—shuffled into the room, pulled himself up with dignity and coughed into his fist.

THE VANISHING BLOODSTAIN

"Madame," he said in his deep melodious voice as he faced Carolyn and looked at her, "I'm very sorry to bother you at this time, but it's the locksmith on the telephone. He insists on talking to you."

"Yes, thank you Benoît," she answered, loud enough for the butler to hear. "Please tell him that I can't come to the phone right now, but I expect him first thing tomorrow morning. Tomorrow's Monday, right?" She asked someone sitting close to her. "Tell him to come equipped to change the locks on every single door on this house. Thank you, Benoît."

People, who are always so nosy about the affairs of others, had gone very quiet. They had heard every word. Then, Carolyn turned to the guests sitting close to her, and explained. "We had a break-in not long ago. I don't want anyone to come into the house again while I'm sleeping upstairs." Carolyn looked at Margo with a self-satisfied grin. Margo chuckled to herself. Carolyn had no idea what a poker face meant.

Chapter 33

The Intruder

A FOYER FULL OF FURNITURE IN A DARK HOUSE next to an oversized stairwell was not going to be the easiest place to trap an intruder, but it was the only one where it could be cornered. If the intruder took the bait, that was. Because this was its last chance to sneak in and find whatever three generations of interlopers had been searching for before the imaginary locksmith showed up to change the locks in the morning.

It had finally stopped raining, and the silence was absolute. Carolyn was hiding in the parlor. Many arguments later, Pierre, Benoît, and Margo, gave up trying to reason with her. She was one stubborn old woman.

"They have been terrorizing me all my life," she said. "I plan to be right here when you capture them." And she refused to budge. She hunkered down on one of the wing back chairs. But it had been a long and sad day with the funeral and the wake, and after a few minutes, Margo heard a soft snoring and knew that Carolyn had fallen asleep.

She wondered how bloody this whole thing was going to get and hoped nobody would get killed. She stood with her Glock behind a column and waited quietly. Pierre had vanished next to a cabinet. Wearing black, he was invisible to the casual eye. Benoît had to sit down. He was too old to squat or stand too long, but Margo had seen him practicing with the surujin in the backyard and had to admit that, of all of them, he was the most lethal contender.

It had been a stressful day, and before she knew it, Margo started to nod off right where she was standing. The sound that alerted her was so soft that she almost thought she had imagined it. But a few seconds later she saw a cloud of fog spread on the floor around the stairwell and a crouching figure in translucent white crawling on the floor by the stairs like a crab. She almost screamed out loud. It was creepy enough that if she hadn't known this was not a ghost, she would have been terrified.

She really hoped that Pierre and Benoît were awake. The plan had called for Margo to utter a piercing cry that would shock the intruder and make it—hopefully—freeze in place, at which point Pierre and Benoît would move in and do their thing. But now, in the dark, Margo had no clue where they were, or even if they were awake at all. She decided to move closer to the intruder.

The Glock was shaking in her hands and she was sweating with fear and anticipation even on this very cold night. She took a few steps, staying behind columns and larger furniture. She was terrified to bump into something and alert the intruder. The fog was disorienting. It was slowly filling the foyer and blurring the lines of the objects around her. With the pistol raised and held by both hands she bumped into someone, and suddenly there was a big strong hand on her mouth. *Shush*, the whisper said, *don't scream.*

The intruder had found a small room under the stairwell and was rummaging in there very quietly. Pierre and Margo moved closer, and Pierre gave a signal into the dark. Movement told her that Benoît was alert and ready. Pierre told her *now*, and she screamed her heart out.

The intruder was shocked. It turned around with a big bang that sounded like a head hitting a wall, and a scuffle ensued. Pierre was throwing punches that were connecting, but he was getting them too.

Agnes Makóczy

Thinking that the perp was trapped, Margo ran to the light switch and turned the lights on. Benoît was a few paces away, and Carolyn sat up in her chair, startled by the sudden lights, and Pierre stood baffled in front of the open room under the stairs. "There's nobody here," he growled with frustration. He scratched his head.

"Outside," Margo yelled, "they must be trying to get away." Benoît—running faster that anyone had ever seen him move—was already at the front door opening it fast as lightning, surujin in hand. "I see a figure in white," he yelled, and went after it, twirling the surujin above his head in the penumbra, barely visible in the meager moonlight.

Margo got to the front door and stepped out in time to hear a heavy swoosh cross the cool air of the night. She looked to the garden between the two houses and saw to her surprise two metal balls sparkle in the dark as they flew circling each other, catching bits of shine from the weak yellow light of the front door. Then, Margo saw the surujin connect with the intruder and tangle in its legs, and after a God-awful scream, go down.

Pierre—baseball bat in hand—ran toward the figure in white, ready to strike if necessary. Margo followed, pointing the Glock upwards to the sky so she wouldn't hurt anyone. But there was no need for histrionics. The intruder had passed out cold on the wet blanket of unpicked autumn leaves. There was a fat branch next to the figure's head. It was obviously what had caused the contusion.

Heart beating a hundred times a minute, Margo breathed deep to center herself. *We did it*, she thought to herself, *thanks to Benoît's surujin. Otherwise, the night would have been a failure.* Pierre looked with awe at the little butler who suddenly seemed a foot taller.

Someone had had the forethought to bring some rope, and Pierre bent down to tie limp wrists behind the perp's back. Then, Margo looked back and saw Carolyn approach with scared steps.

THE VANISHING BLOODSTAIN

"It's okay, Carolyn," Margo told her. "It's safe to come closer. It's not a ghost but a being of flesh and blood dressed like one." They all stared at the ghost on the ground, and Pierre bent down to take the mask off. "Are you ready to find out who's been terrorizing you all this time, Carolyn?" he asked dramatically and yanked the translucent white head cover off.

"Dear God," they heard Carolyn gasp, "it's Denton, Renée's butler! I don't understand! What is he doing here?"

The man had regained consciousness and was furious, struggling against the rope that bound his wrists. Sharmila, awakened by the yelling and the banging of the doors was running toward them with the phone in hand. "Should I call the police?" she asked, but Pierre said, "Oh no, we're going to have a little fun with him first," giving the guy a maleficent grin. The man looked as if he could have killed Pierre on the spot, and Benoît said to leave the surujin around his ankles and to drag him. He looked big enough to defeat all of them. The more incapacitated he was, the better.

It took all of them to drag the miserable man into the house. More rope and silver duct tape finally secured him well enough that they all felt safe that he couldn't run. The man was wheezing. There was a trickle of drying blood and an ugly contusion on his forehead that would leave a scar. He lay there on the rug, moaning, and groaning, and spitting like a dog with rabies. He begged and threatened by turns, but finally calmed down enough to where they sat him up against a wall, and Carolyn managed to get some answers out of him.

"Denton, I don't understand. What are you doing here?"

"Like you didn't know," Denton spat at her furiously.

"No, I don't. I really don't. Are you the one that has been coming in the house at night and scaring me?" she asked. "I was terrified. I thought I was going insane. Why would you do something like this?"

"I was looking for what you father stole."

"You mean what he stole in England? But that was over 100 years ago. How could you possibly know about it? I just found out a couple of days ago."

"You mean you didn't know?"

"About the gold? No, I didn't. I knew he had killed someone important and took off before they could hang him, but that's all I knew. Because he had killed an important person, Margo found references online, and it appears Father took off with something that didn't belong to him. Did the gold belong to your family?" she asked.

"Umm, well, not exactly. It belonged to my great, great grandfather's cousin."

"And..."

"Well, listen, give me a swig of brandy because I'm cold and hurt, and I promise to tell you everything. Then, I hope you'll show mercy and won't call the cops on me." Pierre looked at Benoît who shrugged and went to fetch a bottle of brandy.

"We'll see, Denton. Depends on how good your story is." Pierre pulled up a couple of chairs for Benoît and for Carolyn and they sat down gratefully. Sharmila was sent back to sleep. Pierre and Margo sat on the rug. Once everyone had a swig of brandy, they settled in to find out what the mystery was all about.

"Roderick Bingham was a crook," Denton began, and he looked at his audience. "He seduced Sir John's wife and left her pregnant. Sir John wasn't much into marital duties, and his wife felt lonely. But Sir John was enormously rich. Not only had his family enriched themselves during wars and crusades, but he was a clever man who knew how to invest his money. But he was so busy playing with his treasures that he forgot he had a wife at home.

"Your father—Roderick Bingham—recklessly left Sir John's wife pregnant, and she was going to start showing soon. So they made the decision to steal some coffers with gold coin, which there was plenty of lying around, and they were going to run away to Europe where they would pretend to be husband and wife and start a new life."

"Hold on, Denton. How could you possibly know all that?"

"Because, after the robbery, her maid Maisy told the police. She had helped her mistress pack a bag. At first she was scared to say anything, but the police made her talk."

"Okay, go on."

"Anyway, something went wrong. Sir John must have found out, because suddenly they decided to have the duel. My great, great grandfather was Sir John's Second. Family tradition says that they met on a cold, misty morning in a clearing by the river. He dropped the handkerchief as a signal for the duel to begin, and Sir John and Roderick Bingham took the obligatory ten steps and then turned around to face each other. But they saw the lady, Sir John's wife, run into the clearing screaming, begging them to stop. It was too late. The shots had been fired, and she got caught in the middle. She took one bullet, and Sir John took the other. They both died. And then Roderick Bingham hopped on his horse and vanished with Sir John's gold.

"The family asked my great, great grandfather to go after him and get the thief and the gold back, so he traveled to America, and we have never stopped looking."

"But Denton," Carolyn told him, surprised, "my father didn't come to America. He went to India. I hate to say this, but that's probably the gold he bought the plantation with. I've heard it said that he never became an honorable man until he met my mother. But I think that by then, the gold was gone."

Denton sat there on the floor, dumbstruck. He looked like he had just realized the stupid mistake he had made.

"Besides, Denton," she continued, "surely you didn't think there was any of it left? Not after all this time?"

"Well, a guy can only hope. It's true I haven't found any hidden gold in this house, and I've been looking for a long time. But at least I hoped to find some proof. To maybe convince you to give me some money to keep quiet. Can I get another swig of that brandy?"

"Is that why you were Renée's chauffeur?"

"Yes. To stay close to you."

"Hold on one second," Margo interrupted. "I saw you and Valeria looking all lovey-dovey at each other. You were having an affair, weren't you? If you couldn't find a trace of the treasure yourself, you could always marry her into the family. And then maybe arrange for an accident for Claude and marry her yourself, and get the money obliquely."

"Umm, yes, maybe," grunted Denton. "But I wouldn't have killed Claude. I don't think I could kill anyone. But he was a train wreck waiting to happen. He was mixed up in some serious stuff, so someone was bound to put him away sooner or later."

"Does Valeria know what you've been up to?"

"Oh, yes. She's the one who gave me a copy of your keys."

Margo held her breath and looked at Carolyn. It seemed that she had stopped listening and had missed the last part of Denton's confession. Her eyes were glazed over as if she were somewhere else. Margo knew well what was in her mind. She was reliving all those years of terror when she was a little girl, and when she gave her baby away. Poor Carolyn, how she had paid for her father's sins, never knowing why. She patted the old woman's shaking hand.

"Denton, I have a couple of questions," Margo finally said. "Why the last few weeks? Why not before? Was it the dog?"

"Yes. I tried coming in a few times, but for some reason the dog hated me. He barked at me wherever he saw me. I was afraid he would wake up the whole house."

"And was it your family who terrorized Carolyn when she was a little girl and kidnapped her sister?"

"Yes, that was great grandfather. He came to America thinking Roderick was here. It was by chance that a few years later he saw Roderick's picture in the newspaper. The heiress of this plantation home was coming back to Louisiana with her foreigner husband. She was photographed stepping off the ship in New York, and my great grandfather recognized him. He followed Roderick to Louisiana and terrorized him, hoping to get the gold from him, but your father vanished again."

"What happened to my sister?" asked Carolyn, her voice suddenly quivering.

Denton looked away. Margo wondered if he was as ruthless as he tried to appear because there seemed to be real grief in his eyes. Like Sharmila had inherited the ties of honor that bound her to Parvati's will, Denton seemed to have inherited the obsession and the duty to find the descendants of Roderick Bingham and punish them. But it didn't seem like his heart was in it.

"Carolyn, I'm truly sorry. I heard she died during the kidnapping." Denton, who had been so ruthless and desperate, now just looked like one sad man. "She tried to escape, and one of the men shot her. I'm very sorry. My forebears were a cruel bunch, but not even they would have harmed a child. Your father was a scoundrel, but he didn't deserve such a fate. If it's any consolation, my great grandfather shot the man who did it. Only an animal would have hurt a child. He didn't deserve to live."

Everyone sat around Denton, each of them thinking about their own life. They passed the brandy around again. Margo, who was facing the cathedral window behind the sofa in the parlor, saw that the sun was coming up. What a long night it had been. Closing a case always came with a bit of sadness. Too many skeletons uncovered, and all that.

Agnes Makóczy

Finally, Carolyn struggled up from her chair and said, "Let him go." Funny thing, nobody questioned her. Pierre helped Denton get on his feet and pulled all the duct tape off of him. He cut the cords, and when he was done, patted Denton on the back. Nobody said anything else. There was really nothing left to say. Denton lifted a hand and waved goodbye and stepped through the front door into the new dawn. Last thing Margo remembered was hearing his boots crunch on the pebbles underfoot, on the moist dirt road. She bent down and turned off the little fog machine. It had been out of water for hours.

Someone said they needed a good coffee, and they all headed toward the kitchen. A police siren darted across Kaliste Saloom Road, and some cars honked. It had been a very long night.

Chapter 34

The Gathering

CAROLYN FINALLY ACCEDED to host the gathering. She seemed to be beyond caring, but as Margo told her repeatedly, there still remained the mystery of the death of the beloved grandson. Margo was pretty sure she knew who the culprit was, but you can't just run around accusing people. She wanted everyone in the same room to watch their reactions and to see how they interacted with each other. That way she could make sure that her hunch was right.

When Margo turned in the cigarette butt to the police, they had looked at her with contempt. So a civilian was trying to teach them how to do their job, right? Chances were they wouldn't even have the cigarette butt tested, just because she had brought it in. She tried hard to reason with them. Make them see a connection between Carolyn's and Mutt's poisoning, Renée's death and now Claude's murder, but in the end, she gave up. So her only option was to bully the perp into confessing, or at least into making a mistake.

Carolyn looked like she had aged ten years. Her usually bouncy white curls were limp. Her little linen handkerchief was dirty and wet with tears. She sat lifelessly in her usual rattan chair, staring without interest at the people entering the room. Not even the colorful pillows Sharmila piled up around her made her look any less pale or any less forlorn.

Agnes Makóczy

Margo felt very sorry for her. What she had found out about Denton and his family seemed to have devastated her. That, and the murder of her little sister, and the loss of her baby. It didn't matter one bit that Margo had found her. It was the fifty plus years of her life that had been spent in suffering and loneliness and sorrow. She didn't see her baby grow up. She never dared have another child. In spite of money and later on a happy marriage, Carolyn's life had been empty and lonely. But a murderer had to be stopped, or else it would continue finding excuses to kill more people off. And Carolyn would just have to suffer through it. Who said murder was pretty anyway? People had to stop wanting pretty endings.

The sun-room was full of hostility. Angry whispers floated toward where Margo waited by the doorway, next to Pierre. Everyone was present against their will, all in a sick twisted effort to please Carolyn—who ultimately held their better future in her hands.

Everyone who had been at the Country Club had shown up, except of course for Renée and Claude, now deceased. But in addition to them, Maddy and Sharmila sat to one side, looking out of place, startled to be in the middle of a family event. Maddy wore her unpleasant stone face and stared at Margo from time to time with hatred in her eyes, but Sharmila looked oddly unruffled. Once Margo saw that everyone was settled down, she stepped in front of the gathering and spoke.

"Thank you everyone for coming. I wish it was under more pleasant circumstances. The purpose here is to try to figure out why Carolyn got sick, and Mutt and Renée died of poisoning, and what happened to Claude, and how these events are all connected with a murder that happened in this house almost 60 years ago."

Margo stood by the tall table assigned to her. Sharmila had poured her a generous glass of the ever-present pink lemonade. It was good and tart, and sweet too. She looked at her notes and took a sip of the lemonade. She watched the people staring at her—like cornered animals—with fear in their eyes. She was almost sorry for them.

The sun was pouring in cheerfully through the glass ceiling like this was a celebration, making the lemonade in her glass sparkle, but nobody was smiling. Heaps of fruit and finger food prepared with care for the occasion sat untouched on the table between the two indoor orange trees. It had turned out to be a rather hot day, and a large overhead fan turned lazily around and around, swooshing over their heads, providing a minor amount of cooling breeze, ruffling the tender flowers on the orchids and the paper napkins on the tables.

Carolyn shook her doldrums off and looked at Margo with a tentative smile. She was still dazed by grief, but at least she was making an effort. You don't make it to your 80's if you're not a survivor. For a brief second, Margo had the ugly feeling that Carolyn drew energy from the hostility around her, almost as if she was gloating. She sat in her favorite rattan chair in the warm tropical room like a queen, enjoying unconsciously—she hoped—the power she had over them.

Sharmila, dressed in a purple and gold salwar kameez and gold sandals sat calmly close to Carolyn, her hands folded neatly on her lap, watching the angry people around her. Her hair was nicely picked up in a bun giving her a fresh and friendly appearance. She was wearing gold hoop earrings and even some discreet makeup. There was a new-found peace in Sharmila. She sat with a small contented smile on the chair next to Carolyn.

On the sofa next to Carolyn and to her left sat the Lanes, Sanders and Laura, hunched over sullenly, and wearing clean but simple clothes. Sanders was very nervous, and one of his eyes had a twitch that Margo could see all the way to where she was standing. He darted fearful glances at the people around him like a paranoiac does in a padded cell looking for ghosts in the dark corners.

Laura, his wife, didn't look much better. She hadn't bothered to wear any makeup or even comb her hair properly. It was obvious that she had gotten very little sleep. There were dark circles under her eyes, and there was a foggy sluggishness about her movements as if she were struggling to stay awake.

Next to the Lanes sat Alfred Bailey, Carolyn's attorney and good friend. Alfred Bailey was a mess. He was nervous and restless and sweaty. He looked guilty as hell. His wife Lila sat as far from him on the rattan sofa as distance permitted. Pretty Lila had her arms crossed on her chest, removing herself emotionally from the proceedings. It was hard to believe those two belonged together. Her husband Alfred looked like sheep led to slaughter.

Dr. Schroeder had also aged a lifetime. The three hairs on his bald pate had been carefully combed to the side as if they could make a difference, but they were dirty, greasy hairs, and the pate was shiny with sweat. He kept wiping his forehead with a soiled and wrinkled handkerchief. There were wet patches around his armpits, and beads of sweat above his lips. His wife Bernice, wearing animal-print tights, stiletto high heels, and an excessively youthful looking tight black sweater, sat in stony silence looking straight ahead, determined to make no eye contact with anyone, while the good doctor fidgeted with his glasses and couldn't sit still.

Margo thought about all these people who didn't want to be where they were. But they all had to please Carolyn under penalty of being disinherited. Carolyn, without any malicious intent—at least consciously—exerted great control over the people around her, and Margo was glad she wasn't in their shoes. It was probably a full-time job, keeping the rich woman pleased.

Maddy had to be threatened to attend the gathering, and after a lot of complaining, and seeing how she would lose her job if she didn't, she finally turned up. But she wasn't happy. Her arms were crossed over her chest, and her pouty mouth declared to the world that she was protesting. She threw ugly, belligerent looks at Margo, which Margo simply ignored. She was standing behind the little rattan love seat where Dolly and Dotty sat together like two peas in a pod, looking confused, as if they had no clue what was going on. But Margo knew well enough that they were neither senile, nor as confused as they tried to appear. She had discovered early on that those two could be pretty devious, and in one instance at least, pretty cruel as well.

Parvati and her insignificant husband arrived with fanfare. Parvati agitated her cheap metal bracelets annoying everyone. She loudly let everyone know that she was offended, and she and Matt refused to sit. Matt stood meekly by her, looking like he wished the earth would swallow him already. There was an air of resentful indignation about them, but the threats implied in Margo's welcome speech had calmed them into submission, and so they stood by one of the potted orange trees with the bitterness written all over their faces. Well, if they refused to sit, that was their business, but once the dirt started hitting the fan, their legs would get weak enough and buckle, and they would come to regret their decision.

And then there was cold and aloof Valeria. All dressed in mourning black for someone that she didn't even love, she had quietly stepped into the room at the appointed time without telling anyone hello and vanished into the back of the room like a chameleon. There was not a speck of sorrow about her, even though Claude had died barely a few days earlier. And Margo wondered how Carolyn had managed to get her to show up since there was no family tie left between them. Finally, everyone settled down, and an ominous silence fell over the cheerless group.

"So we'll call this meeting to order. Before I begin, there's one last thing. The back door has been locked, so if you're going to try to walk out before this meeting is adjourned, that's not going to work."

Agnes Makóczy

She looked to her left and saw Pierre standing solidly by the other door. She sighed and then started talking.

"This all began when Carolyn's friend Father Armand came to visit her from Half Moon Bay. Carolyn had been an old parishioner of his, and when he came to visit her he had no idea it was her 80th birthday and that she was having a party.

"At the party he met Parvati, the long lost Indian niece, daughter of Carolyn's much younger sister, and her husband Matt of whom nobody knows much of anything mainly because he's always so quiet. This was a great surprise for Carolyn. After all, she had no idea that her estranged niece had any interest in living close to her. Carolyn has mentioned a number of times that she herself has never had any children.

"Carolyn tells Father Armand that Sanders and Laura Lane are coming. Father Armand already knows them well. He told me that Sanders used to be a senator. There were a number of scandals tied to the time when he served. As it often happens in politics, that was all swept under the rug and forgotten. The Lanes live next door to Carolyn.

"Father Armand also knows Dolly, Dotty, and Renée. They also had been parishioners of his. You see, they all attended the same church while Father Armand still lived in Lafayette. The four old ladies were in charge of the flower committee together. They are also lifelong friends. They have known each other since college and share many secrets. Dolly and Dotty live in a Youngsville nursing home where Renée also lived before she died. They have always looked like sisters, and they could easily be mistaken for one another.

"Then, there is Claude—the favorite—the beloved grandson who could do no wrong, who stood to inherit the bulk of everything Carolyn had on earth, and who was the child of her deceased husband's only child, from a previous marriage. Claude recently showed up with a quiet girl, Valeria, about whom nothing much is known. Even though they were engaged, it never looked like they had any affection for each other.

"So, let's talk about Alfred Bailey. Nice guy, socially rather awkward and undependable. He grew up poor, and through great personal effort made it through law school. He married up, way up, to a young and lovely girl with a whole lot of money. There was a financial scandal of international ramifications. But they never could prove anything against him, and they ended up dropping the charges.

"Now here we have Dr. Schroeder. Carolyn's husband died under his care. He's not what you would call a skilled doctor, and people have had their doubts about the death of his friend, Carolyn's husband, but he's never been formally accused, nor has there ever been an autopsy. In a town ruled by the good old boys, little accidents can easily be swept under the rug. Dr. Schroeder also has a younger wife—as a matter of fact, a much younger wife. She is ambitious, as you all know.

"So here we are at Carolyn's party. Family stories are being rehashed, and Renée mentions the bloody rug and an old murder. Something she said must have startled a murderer in the room because suddenly Carolyn is lying on the floor in a dead faint, clutching her throat. Mutt, her poor dog who ran into the room and lapped up most of her champagne, is found dead under the bushes two days later. The veterinarian says he's been poisoned.

"But before all this, Carolyn recklessly mentions during the party that same day that she's changing her will, and fears of being disinherited spread among the guests. This too is an enormous motivator. Some people in this room already knew about the will beforehand and could have come prepared with a poison that's easy enough to obtain online. Anyway, Carolyn survives.

"She comes back from the hospital convinced that it was nothing but a minor heart episode. And this is when strange things begin to happen. Sharmila her maid has managed to clean the infamous rug that now sits pristine clean in the foyer. But Carolyn comes down one morning and sees that the blood stain is back. She's obviously horrified.

"Meantime, paintings, statues, and other objects, randomly move in the middle of the night by themselves, and they're driving Carolyn crazy. She thinks she's hallucinating and that there's something seriously wrong with her. It gets to the point that a few weeks later she's is easily convinced by her loved ones—and I use the term loosely—she's convinced to check herself into Dr. Schroeder's sanitarium.

"Now let me tell you quickly about the mysterious blood stain. Carolyn and everyone else have gotten used to it as it has never come out. But one day, the new housekeeper Sharmila brings in a pail of soapy water, and with a minor effort, manages to make the stubborn stain simply vanish. Carolyn is so pleased that she happily adds Sharmila to the will thinking here's a housekeeper to keep forever, plus there's this bond between them anyway due to the fact that they were both born in India. You have to understand that Carolyn has so much money that she doesn't know what to do with it. And she's a generous woman and gladly adds people to her will. After all, she doesn't have any children of her own, and she has to leave the money to someone.

"But Sharmila, in spite of this kindness, proceeds to play some ugly games on Carolyn. At times, the bloody rug reappears and remains there for days, and then Sharmila pretends to clean it again, and the bloodstain vanishes. It's a very cruel prank that disturbs Carolyn very much. When Lucy and I explored the attic we found the twin of the rug. It looks exactly the same in design and size. They were obviously acquired together as part of a set. Either Sharmila or Parvati must have come across this clean rug stored in the attic while snooping, and gotten the idea to substitute one for the other.

THE VANISHING BLOODSTAIN

"Whenever Sharmila put the bloody rug out, she smeared some animal blood on it to make it look fresh." Margo watched the shocked and disgusted faces of the guests. "I know. It's repulsive. I smelled it and touched it, and it was really blood. It was also Sharmila who was moving things around the house while the older woman slept, and Carolyn—who is no longer young—thought she was going nuts. Now why would someone—who looks as reputable and nice as Sharmila— do such a horrible thing to her employer who has been nothing but kind to her?"

Sharmila looked pointedly at Margo, blushing furiously.

"Do you want to tell us the truth, Sharmila? Or should I?"

Sharmila shook her head. She was fidgeting with the gold thread on her shirt, pulling at it nervously. "You tell them," she said quietly.

"All right then. Parvati wanted to drive her aunt insane. She got the idea when visiting Dona Paula Beach—on the island of Goa—with her husband. The daughter of Goa's Viceroy jumps to her death off a cliff and now haunts the place. After this, the cliff becomes a well-known suicide landmark. It was in the news recently that a young man drove his stepmother insane and made her jump off the same cliff so that he could inherit her fortune. We've all heard the story. She's repeated it a number of times.

"When I read up on the story on the internet, I realized that that was where Parvati had gotten the idea. She decides to drive Carolyn insane with the help of Sharmila. Not completely nuts, you understand, just enough to have her declared incompetent and get power of guardianship over her affairs. Of course, if Carolyn dies of a heart attack, it wouldn't be the end of the world. It would save her the trouble of the paperwork. She would still inherit enough to live the rest of her life in comfort. So she blackmails Sharmila into playing those horrible tricks on the woman who has been nothing but kind to her. Parvati didn't want to get her hands dirty."

"Did you, Parvati?" Margo asked, looking at the young woman shaking with anger. "Why not let someone else do the dirty work for you, right?" Parvati took a step toward Margo as if she was about to attack her, but Matt grabbed her arm and whispered something in her ear. Parvati stood down, but continued staring at Margo with hatred.

"Now don't look at me with so much indignation, Parvati. Sharmila has already told me everything. You wanted clean and easy. And you almost succeeded. Had Father Armand not asked me to look into this, you and your husband would have slowly driven her insane. The thing is, Parvati, that you're not so smart. Someone cleverer than you must have helped you to put the plan in place."

"Matt," Margo said turning to the husband that had shriveled against the orange tree like he wanted to vanish. "Tell us, Matt, what do you do for a living?"

Everyone turned toward Matt and stared. All he did was stutter.

"That's right, Matt. You don't work for a living, because this kindly old lady is giving you and your wife enough money to live on. Okay, let me rephrase the question. What is your profession? And speak up please, so everyone can hear you."

"Psychiatrist. I'm a psychiatrist," Matt said meekly looking at his feet. Parvati was furious. She looked cornered and mean. She glared at Carolyn without a speck of fondness. Margo wondered what had caused the young woman to hate her elderly aunt so much.

"Ah! So you would know well enough how to play with someone's mind and drive them insane. And so, instead of being grateful to your wife's aunt for her kindness, you decide, what the heck, let's just take it all."

"Yes," Parvati said angrily. "Because I hate her. I hate her." As Parvati screamed, the saliva spritzed out of her mouth and she kept wiping it off with her arm. "You all think she's so wonderful and so loving. But it's not true. She's a cruel, manipulative woman."

"What are you talking about, Parvati?" Carolyn stood up, surprised, helped up by Sharmila. "What have I ever done to you? Why would you hate me?"

"I hate you because you have this big beautiful house and all the money in the world. Because I see that you have everything you want and yet your sister lives in poverty like a pariah. You keep saying that your mother and father had this fairy tale life in India, but it's not true. They died penniless, and you never even bothered to visit them. The natives took everything away from them and ostracized them, and my mother grew up in poverty—and so did I, while you lived this grand life. And now you throw me crumbs. What am I supposed to do with them? Pack them up and send them to my mother?"

"Parvati," protested Carolyn. "I had no idea. Of course I wrote. I wrote all the time and tried to get them to come live here. But Father refused."

"Well, he was as selfish as you are then, because that horrible climate cost your mother her life."

"I begged them to come. I begged your mother to come as well, but she refused."

"She refused because she didn't want your charity."

"She refused because she never liked me. And because she loved India and couldn't bear the thought of leaving."

"That's not true, Carolyn. We were as poor as street dogs. Matt and I saved up for years to put the trip money together."

"Why didn't you ask me?"

"Because you would have said no."

"How can you say that? I've been so lonely in this house by myself all these years. I would have loved for you and your mother to move in with me. I would have loved it." Carolyn sat back down. She was crying again, but not a tear was running Parvati's cheeks. In a hostile display of hatred, her arms were crossed on her chest, and she looked around the room as if daring anyone to say anything. The guests avoided eye contact with her, and all turned toward Margo who continued her report.

"Now the question remains: how did you talk Sharmila into helping you? She carried that cumbersome rug up and down from the attic while her employer slept. She stayed up half the night moving things around the house to confuse Carolyn.

"How did you manage that, Parvati? You blackmailed poor Sharmila into doing your bidding because she owed you a debt of honor. And once you became Carolyn's legal guardian, you would be able to do whatever you pleased with her fortune. It was really worth the effort. For a brief moment, I even thought that it had been you two who had killed Claude to get the principal heir out of the way. But I digress.

"It turns out that I noticed that Sharmila calls Carolyn Shrimati, which in her country is a customary sign of respect toward an older woman, but she calls Parvati Priya. Now Priya is a name, but it is also a term of affection like "dear" or "beloved". It occurred to me that normally, a seemingly honest person like Sharmila wouldn't call her blackmailer that. There had to be a reason. I found out that Sharmila owes her life and her mother's life to Parvati's father. This is the bond between the two women, and Sharmila is honor-bound to do whatever Parvati asks of her. When Parvati decided to enlist Sharmila's help to drive Carolyn insane, Sharmila had no choice."

Chapter 35

The Baileys And The Lanes

"WE PROCEED. SANDERS AND LAURA LANE, you two have all kinds of skeletons in your closet, don't you? A couple of nights ago, Brooks and I saw you barbequing documents in an oil drum on your back porch. I presume they pertain to that scandal you were involved in back when you served in the Senate. You've been begging Carolyn for that piece of land on the other side of the road. It's easily four acres large, right?" The Lanes nodded obediently. They were red as beets.

"I wondered why you were so intent on getting your hands on it. A couple of things jumped out of the page when I was doing my research. A Texas company wants to build a series of condos right there. It will have a playground, swimming pool, fancy apartments, the works. Whoever owns the land will get a pretty penny if he's willing to sell. Now, if that land was yours, I bet you'd be more than happy to sell.

"Then, there's the state of your finances. You two are broke. You wear the same clothes all the time. Not because you don't have any imagination, as Lila thinks, but because you don't have the money to buy new ones. Am I right? You've been blackmailed for a long time and have been bled dry, haven't you? So, I just wondered whether you two would have the guts to try to murder your neighbor to inherit faster and then get rid of your blackmailer."

Agnes Makóczy

"I could never hurt anyone," Sanders said, getting up from his chair all agitated and looking at the guests with a begging tone of voice. The twitch in his eye seemed to have gotten worse. "Ask Carolyn. She knows we're decent people. Maybe I made some mistakes when I was a senator, but I stepped down, and I've accepted the consequences." Then he looked at Margo. "I would never murder anyone."

"I believe you. It's not that easy to murder someone. Or at least I should say it's not that easy for a civilized person to murder another one. Besides, Renée's death didn't fit in, unless she drank the poison destined for Carolyn. But two more people came to visit the Lanes while Brooks and I were watching," Margo told the squirmy crowd. "One of them was Alfred."

"Alfred," Margo asked him as she turned to face him. "What were you doing at the Lanes'?"

To everyone's surprise Lila had suddenly jumped up from the sofa as if someone had pulled her up by a string. And she yelled at Alfred. She was furious. She had her fists on her hips and looked like she was going to whack her husband.

"You little twit. You went anyway. I told you to leave it alone. I've told you a hundred times that these people are trouble." Lila turned at the other guests and then to Margo. "He's a good man," she said. "He's a good man who does stupid things because he loves me." She looked at her husband again. She was angry, but there was a lot of fondness in her eyes as well.

"Why did you go see the Lanes, Alfred?" Margo insisted, suspecting the answer already. "Why?"

"Tell her Alfred, or I'll tell her." Lila looked exasperated. "Speak, you fool."

"Well, it was like this," Alfred finally said, squirming in his seat. "We were all being blackmailed. If we didn't pay out, Carolyn was going to find out how worthless we were, and she would cut us out of the will. We were going to try to get rid of him."

"What I don't understand," Lila told her husband, her voice getting louder and louder, "is what you needed that money for. I have plenty of it, plenty enough for the both of us. I knew what a poor kid you were when we met. I knew you would never amount to much. You're too much of a softy to be a good attorney. But did I care? No. I didn't care because I loved you, and I don't care today because I still do." In all this, Alfred was watching his pretty wife with awe in his eyes. These two were going to be okay.

"Okay, you two. Sit down. We still have a lot of ground to cover. Miss Carolyn, things are going to get more painful from here on. Would you rather not be here?"

"No, my dear. I need to know the truth. Hear it for myself. I'd rather stay."

"Do you need a break?"

"No, no. Let's get it over with."

"Okay, then. Dolly and Dotty. What struck me from the start was that you two are so alike. Lucy and I found many interesting things in the attic. One of them was a photo album of all four of you friends holding babies. It was hard to know which one was Dolly and which one was Dotty. Until I remembered what Lila told me, that is. Dolly, you're always wearing a brooch. She mentioned that you have a number of them and never go anywhere without wearing one.

"These pictures show the passage of time. You all get older, and your children are shown growing up. There are many pictures of Dolly and her brooch, Dolly and her brooch and her daughter, and then Dolly and her brooch and her grand-daughter. Finally there's one where the grand-daughter is old enough to be recognized. It's you, Valeria." Everyone gasped and looked at the girl trying to blend in with the potted orange tree. She was as pale as a ghost.

"Valeria is Dolly's grand-daughter. Somehow she managed to meet Claude, and got him to propose. Mind you, some girls know how to do that. She must have wanted to marry into the family. There was just so much money, and you Dolly don't have any left, do you? Lila mentioned that you don't have two pennies to rub together. Maybe you never had as much as your friends did. I bet that nursing home is extremely expensive as well. A call to the director of the nursing home confirmed that you're behind on your bills. Everyone has a chauffeur. Dotty does, Carolyn does, Renée did, but you don't. It's not because you don't want one, but because you can't afford one, isn't it true?"

"Why, Dolly, why?" Carolyn said, the shock making her voice shake. "If you needed money, why didn't you just tell me?"

"Because I was ashamed, that's why," Dolly's small voice answered bitterly. She looked at her worn-out shoes. Margo had never noticed how worn they were. "You always had so much money, and so did Dotty and Renée. You all never noticed how hard it was for me to keep up with you, the trips, the nice clothes. I had barely any money left to eat. But you all never cared."

"Don't say that. I would have given you all the money you needed. I have more than I know what to do with. You should have come to me. To cause all this trouble and heartache for such a small thing."

"But it's not a small thing," Margo interrupted. "For you Carolyn it might be a small thing because you have so much of it. But in Dolly's heart, the envy and the jealousy festered and grew with time. Didn't it, Dolly?" Dolly was looking away, avoiding eye contact. "Greed has been eating away at your friend for years. She passed on that greed to her grand-daughter who found the idea of acquiring your money almost rightful and fair."

"Now, was it your idea to send in Valeria? Or was it hers all alone? Well, who cares, really? And please, someone stop me if I'm wrong. The point is that you were probably tired of being poor, and Valeria was terrified that she was going to be left with nothing but your debts. So, she seduced Claude and managed to get a proposal out of him." Margo looked at Valeria pointedly. "Did you promise to help him get at Auntie's money faster? Auntie, who so badly wanted to see Claude with babies before she died?" Valeria didn't answer, but her look said it all.

"And then—because that wasn't enough—they convinced Maddy somehow to spy on the family so she could find out how things were going. Okay, I have to be honest. At first, I thought Maddy was related to Dolly, because of the brooch. Who wears those anymore?

"When I first arrived, I came across a photograph of Maddy in which she's wearing a brooch similar to those that Dolly wears. It looked expensive too, and oversized and old fashioned, and not something a young woman who helps clean houses would wear. It had to be more than a coincidence. How did she get it? She was either related to her, or had received it as a gift or payment. Then, when I found out that they weren't related, there was only one explanation left. Dolly had to be very grateful to give one of her precious brooches away.

"Having Maddy here was very convenient. After all, they couldn't be in this house seven days a week. Claude tried to move in, but Carolyn didn't let him. So, Maddy reported on the comings and goings of everyone. Then, unexpectedly, Maddy fell in love with Pierre." She looked at the chauffeur, so tall, dark, and handsome, and wasn't surprised. Pierre looked flustered. Obviously he had no idea that Maddy had a crush on him. Margo chuckled to herself. Men!

"Maddy gave Pierre her phone number written on the back of a photograph of her which my cats found in his house when Brooks was staying there. That's how I found out about that. The paper with the phone number was crumpled, and it had been thrown away."

Agnes Makóczy

"Did I get it right, Maddy?" she asked. Maddy had her stone face on, the one that showed no expression. Margo knew what unrequited love looked like, and this was it. Margo took a sip of lemonade.

Chapter 36

Maddy

"AND NOW, LET'S GET TO THE MURDERS. Miss Carolyn, I suspect that Claude signed his own death warrant by pushing someone too far. He was blackmailing not only Alfred and the Lanes, but just about everyone in this room. He might have been genuinely fond of you, but he had no scruples about squeezing money out of people. And he might have even been desperate enough to get to yours as well. We'll never know what kind of shady deals he was involved in that might have pressured him into getting his hands on money fast."

"How can you say something like that, Margo?" she asked, hurt at the accusations against her beloved Claude.

"Carolyn, surely you noticed that Claude was not very honest. But as a doting grandmother, you probably looked the other way."

"Oh, I don't know," she said looking away. "Maybe sometimes I had my doubts about him, but he was so sweet and caring." She put her hand on her chest as if she were trying to calm her heart. "But blackmail? I'm having a hard time accepting that my Claude was capable of anything like that. But if it's true that he was blackmailing Alfred and the Lanes, they could be the ones who killed him. Alfred said they were going to get rid of him."

"But not by murdering him, Carolyn," Alfred protested. "How could you even imagine that we could kill him? We were going to pay him off in one big lump sum, or if that failed, we were going to go to the police and confess. The whole thing was becoming unbearable."

"Well, someone did murder him," she cried stubbornly, "and that someone is in this room. I know it." Carolyn leaned over Sharmila's shoulder and sobbed. It was heart-wrenching. Suddenly, everyone was talking. The Lanes got into an argument with Alfred, and Lila was trying to separate them. Parvati and her husband Matt hurried over to where Carolyn was sitting with Sharmila and were standing in front of her, gesticulating wildly, trying to explain themselves. But the old lady just shook her head. She looked devastated. Dr. Schroeder and his wife had moved to a corner and were having a heated argument sotto voce. They knew they were up next. Margo was watching them, wondering if they were going to try to make a run for it.

But it was Maddy alone who attempted the run. She had slowly inched herself toward the door where Pierre stood guard, taking opportunity of the sudden chaos. She was about to put her hand on the door handle and slip out when Pierre grabbed her by the arm. "Go back and sit down, Maddy," he ordered. Maddy begged and cajoled, but Pierre stood firm. Then she got angry and yanked her arm out of Pierre's grasp and went back to where she'd been standing before. Margo yelled for order. This was a mob scene and people refused to quieten down. Finally, Pierre whistled loudly, and that got everyone's attention. They went back to their seats meekly and sat down. Parvati, Matt and Valeria skulked at the back of the room like children in time-out.

"Thank you for not leaving, Maddy," Margo said, "Because I have a bone to pick with you. You ran me off the road the other day and almost managed to kill Lucy and me."

Maddy stepped forward, red in the face with indignation. "No, I didn't. Why would I want to run you off the road?" She put her fists on her hips and looked at Margo with hostility.

"Oh, I don't know. Maybe because you didn't want us to reach the nursing home? Maybe you didn't want us to find out who Valeria really is, and why she was engaged to Claude? Or maybe you didn't want us to find out that you're a spy, and that Valeria and Dolly are the ones who hired you?"

"How did you know it was me?" Maddy asked with a touch of fear in her voice.

"It had to be you, Maddy. I saw a beat up green truck in the driveway that day. Dr. Schroeder drives a fancy black car. Claude did as well. No way would someone like Claude have been caught dead in a beat up pickup truck. Parvati and the Lanes are close to bankrupt and have small passenger cars, and neither Benoît nor the cook would want to hurt me, I don't think. And I was driving Pierre's car. So there was only you left. I remember the look you gave me when I came back after the accident. Everyone looked worried sick, except you. You weren't even surprised. It had to be you."

"Well, you can't prove anything."

"I beg to differ, Maddy. The car that I almost hit when I was sliding off the road was full of teenagers. The parents were too busy and terrified trying to avoid the accident. But the kids were having the time of their lives. They took a picture of your license plate with their cellphone. Kids nowadays are clever like that. They learn it from TV shows. When they came back to rescue me from the ravine, they gave the police the information. And guess what? We found out that the nasty green pickup truck that almost killed us is registered to your brother. Now the question is whether it was you who was driving it or was it your brother."

While Margo talked, Maddy had approached and was now up in her face, standing so close that Margo could smell the pink lemonade on her breath. "I hate you," she screamed. "I hate you, I hate you."

"But why would you hate me, Maddy?"

Agnes Makóczy

"I hate you because you took my boyfriend away from me," she screamed, completely out of control. It was Margo's turn to look baffled. "Pierre loved me until you got here, and now he only has eyes for you. I hate you." Pierre and Margo looked at each other, and Pierre shrugged. "I wanted to get rid of you. I didn't want to kill you, but I wanted to scare you away so you would go home." During Maddy's outburst, there had been a deadly silence in the room. Everyone was shocked. And then Maddy started crying. She hugged herself and bent her head down and the tears were coming so fast that they were plopping on the floor tile.

Margo sighed. She went and hugged Maddy and patted her gently on the back. "Don't cry, Maddy. He's not in love with me, and I didn't take him away from you. Come on, let's find you a seat. Don't cry, now."

Chapter 37

The Murders

MARGO WAS SPEAKING TO A HUMBLED AUDIENCE. It seemed that the rebellion and indignation had fizzled out of them, and now they were just a bunch of frightened perps with greater or lesser nooses around their necks. Maddy was in trouble for road rage. Parvati and Matt were going to be charged with something as well, unless Carolyn refused to press charges. Sharmila had acted out of duty and honor. It was the way of foreigners, and it was understandable. She was the easiest to forgive. But Valeria had conspired to help unburden a harmless old woman of her money. Even if Carolyn didn't press charges, her friendship with Dolly was over. As to Sanders and Laura Lane and to their buddy Alfred, they hadn't really done anything illegal. Their financial shenanigans were all in the past, and other than conspiring like fools, they had done no harm.

"Everyone please take a seat and stop talking. It's time to solve the murders. Thank you. It was on Carolyn's 80th birthday that Renée first looked at Dr. Schroeder and told him that he looked familiar. It is a known fact that—as you get older—memories of your youth become more vivid than memories of what you have experienced just ten minutes ago. Why did Dr. Schroeder seem familiar to her? He was not her doctor and hadn't seen him in many years. She remembered him because of the party. He was at the famous party where someone got killed.

"Carolyn mentioned that Sharmila had gotten rid of the famous bloodstain. In free association, that reminded Renée of the murder of Johnny Lagasse that had happened over fifty years earlier in the foyer of this same house. Johnny bled out on the rug after dying mysteriously during a party which was attended by the four friends as well as Dr. Schroeder, while they were all still in college. They were all drunk and didn't remember what had happened at the party. But Renée must have witnessed it and been too drunk to remember at the time. It wasn't until the day of the birthday party that she put the bloody rug, the murder, and the familiar face of Dr. Schroeder together.

"There had been a lot of drinking that night. Everyone went home and slept it off. The next morning a maid discovered Johnny's body in the foyer, his blood spilled on the rug, his face beaten to a bloody pulp. The only way they managed to identify him was by his identification papers, which were in his pocket."

"So are you saying that Dr. Schroeder killed that boy at the party?" Dotty asked, horrified, "Our Dr. Schroeder?"

"Yes, I'm afraid so. There can be no other explanation. The original Dr. Schroeder was a brilliant young scientist. Yet all I hear from everyone is that the Dr. Schroeder of today is incompetent and negligent. How could that be possible? Only if your Dr. Schroeder was not the original one.

"Back then it was easy to steal someone's identity. They must have been of similar weight, height, and general appearance. All Dr. Schroeder had to do was switch identification papers. And he got away with it. He walked away with the real Dr. Schroeder's inheritance and built the sanitarium. Until Renée recognized him, that is.

"That's when Dr. Schroeder got scared. Renée was so insistent that he seemed familiar. What if she remembered more of the story? What if she remembered him standing over the body of Johnny Lagasse? What if Renée remembered that the dead boy was not Johnny

Lagasse at all, but Desmond Schroeder, young rising medical star without a family but with an enormous trust fund?

"Renée was in a chatty mood. He had to put an end to that, and quickly. He took some Sodium Nitroprusside from his medical bag, which he always has with him, and added some to one glass of champagne. But the four friends were always taking each other's drinks away. Somehow, in the confusion, Carolyn ended up with Renée's champagne and sipped on it. The rest is history. She had a small sip. Then Mutt came bolting in and jumped on her, making her spill the poison. And all excited by the company and the confusion, the dog lapped it up and went outside and died. They found him under a bush behind the house while Carolyn was at the hospital recuperating. I wanted to know what Mutt died of, so I went to the veterinarian. He was the one who explained the poison to me. "

"But why was he carrying poison around?" someone asked. "He didn't know he was going to kill her the first time, did he?"

"Fair question. Sodium Nitroprusside is often found in doctors' medical bags because it can be used to measure urine ketone bodies as a follow up for diabetic patients. It's also used in emergency situations to rapidly decrease high blood pressure. It's a red colored sodium salt that would have dissolved in the champagne making it ever so slightly redder, but basically invisible. Dr. Schroeder would have gotten away with it."

"If Carolyn had not picked up Renée's glass."

"Exactly. Dr. Schroeder—or I should say Johnny Lagasse—studied chemistry. He knew exactly what he was doing. Then, when he saw that he had failed, he knew he had to try again. This time he had to make sure he got things right. He held on to Renée's poisoned fruit juice and made sure she was the one who drank it."

Agnes Makóczy

"Why, Dr. Schroeder?" Dotty asked, shocked and horrified. "Why did you have to kill her? She was just an old fool like the rest of us. She was rambling. She would have never remembered."

"He couldn't take the risk, Dotty. He had to make sure she wouldn't talk. The sad thing for him is that Sharmila never did make the bloodstain vanish. When they examine the DNA on it—if they ever do—they might still be able to compare it to the dead boy's relatives. They will discover soon enough who the real dead man is. And there's no statute of limitations on murder in Louisiana. I'm afraid that greed got the best of our good doctor."

"It wasn't greed," the old doctor said, his bald pate glistening with beads of sweat. He took his large white handkerchief and mopped his brow again. "You don't understand. Desmond Schroeder was oblivious of his good fortune. He threw his money around like he didn't have a care in the world. It didn't matter how much he spent, there was always more where it came from. He had houses, he had cars, and he had that fancy diploma. I had nothing. I struggled in school, but he always excelled. I kept repeating classes because I couldn't pass them, but he graduated early. He was so damn smart.

"I was always in financial trouble, so he invited me to live with him. It made him feel superior that he was helping me out, paying for my tuition and such. Always there with a handout, and he never let me forget it. He constantly rubbed my nose in it."

"But he sounds like he was also a generous young man and a good friend. He paid for your tuition. You lived in his house. How could that have been such a bad thing? How could that have justified murder, Doctor?"

"You don't understand, Miss Fontaine. It's true that he did all that, but it came with a price. He was constantly throwing his superiority in my face. 'Work harder, Johnny,' he would say. 'Study harder, Johnny. Don't drink so much, Johnny. Don't waste your time or you'll never get anywhere in life, Johnny.' He drove me nuts with his nagging. I couldn't take it any longer. When we drove back together to Lafayette after his graduation, and we had this crazy party in this house, and he got drunk and fell down, I had this idea, this incredible idea. I could become Dr. Schroeder, and Johnny Lagasse would die. The loser would die. He was completely passed out on the floor. He wasn't used to drinking. I picked him up and threw him face down against the fireplace stoop. When his face hit the red bricks he was so disfigured his mother wouldn't have recognized him had she been alive. Who was a loser now, huh?"

"He considered you his friend."

"He was a conceited jerk," the doctor said and looked away. The pompous air had gone out of him and now there he sat, defeated, just an old man.

Margo looked at the bewildered guests staring at Dr. Schroeder. Most of them had acted with malicious intent, but none of them would have been capable of murder. When she had gone down the list of suspects, she had realized that only Dr. Schroeder could have had the opportunity and the motive to kill.

"Then, the blackmail began," she continued. "Once Claude realized how easy it was to blackmail Alfred and the Lanes, he tried it out on Dr. Schroeder. I saw them a number of times together, arguing, Claude talking agressively and Dr. Schroeder smoking with shaking hands."

"So Dr. Schroeder killed Claude as well?" Dotty asked. "Because of the blackmail?"

"Yes, Dotty. He agreed to meet him at the Country Club by the golf course and gave him a poisoned cigarette. You know how smokers are, they offer each other cigarettes. Dr. Schroeder smokes expensive stuff, and Claude would have been happy to accept one. Tests will prove it's the same poison. Deadly when inhaled. Right, doctor?" Dr.

Schroeder looked away and didn't answer. "Claude tossed the cigarette stub under the bushes, like he always did, which was where I found it. The police have it now. They're running tests. Finally."

In all this, Bernice Schroeder had gotten up from the love seat and started inching away from her husband. Until then, she hadn't said a word. She kept shaking her head. "This isn't happening. How could you do this, Desmond? You've ruined everything. All these people dead. What were you thinking about?"

"I was thinking of us. Claude was ruining us. I had no money left to give him. You would have lost your house and your pretty car, and everything we've worked so hard to build." He was walking toward her with his arms stretched out, trying to hold her. But she kept walking backward.

"Don't touch me, you monster. I can't believe it. What makes you think that these things were so important to me? I used to work in a bar when you met me, for heaven's sake. Just not having to go back there to work and be groped by drunk, disgusting men, was enough to make me happy. I didn't need a pretty house. Any house would have been better that the shack I used to live in. Any car would have been good enough as long as it worked. Get away from me you horrible freak. I never want to talk to you again." Bernice walked to the door and stood by Pierre, with her arms across her chest, sobbing to herself.

Lila had finally recovered enough from the shock to ask a question. "But Margo, how on earth did you figure all this out?"

"It was a number of details put together. It took Claude many hours to die. When Ernesto—the young man at the Country Club— found him, he said a last few words. The young man, wanting to make sure he wouldn't forget them, scribbled them down. He was going to tell the police, but they were rude to him and pushed him to the side. So when I went to the club to talk to him, young Ernesto gave me the paper. It was very cryptic. It said *because of the rug* and then he repeated himself and said *because of the stupid rug*. Ernesto was absolutely sure that those were his exact words."

"So," Lila jumped in, "you put together an old murder, a bloody rug, witnesses and a young man's last words and concluded that?"

"Almost," Margo answered. "I did a lot of research. Claude made tons of phone calls to the doctor's cell phone. He went to visit him at the sanitarium, and the nurses said they had heard them argue bitterly a number of times. He also visited the Lanes. Brooks and I were there when your husband and the Lanes were being threatened by him. I recognized his voice. I'm a musician. I have a good ear for timbre. Besides, neither your husband nor the Lanes would have had the guts to kill him. It had to be the doctor, who had already killed twice before."

"That's not possible," Carolyn wailed. "He was such a sweet young man."

"He was no sweet young man, Carolyn," the doctor answered. "He was a greedy little bastard. He saw me pour the Sodium Nitroprusside salts in your champagne and realized what was going on. He was a clever young man, your sweet Claude. He started blackmailing me, and he watched me like a hawk. When he saw me give poisoned juice to Renée, he became very greedy. He had one attempted murder and now one murder on me. There was no satisfying him, Carolyn. I gave him every penny I had, and when all that was gone, I had to do something."

"You're a monster, Schroeder," Carolyn cried.

"I was just trying to save myself."

Everyone in the room had quietened down, overwhelmed by what had just happened. When Benoît stepped into the sun-room to announce the police, the guests barely reacted. Maybe they thought everyone was going to jail. But they only took Dr. Schroeder. Margo watched him go meekly with his head hanging, and wondered what it could feel like to live a life of lies and deceit and never be able to tell anyone.

Epilogue

Farewell

MARGO CAME DOWNSTAIRS WITH HER LUGGAGE. She was almost ready to go. Carolyn was standing in front of the fireplace in the parlor. Margo put her bags by the front door and approached her. She was holding an old sepia photograph, looking at it through the light coming in from the cathedral window. She handed it to Margo and pointed to the young woman and the slightly older man smiling at the camera. Behind them, she could see a muddy river chock full of barges and dinghies and people in native garb, carrying bundles on their backs and heads, toiling away, long forgotten.

"Look at how handsome they were, my father, the Englishman, and his beautiful Cajun wife. He built his plantation and the timber company in Upper Burma with the stolen gold of the man he killed, and that of his lover and child. He was a charmer, my father, but he was a crook, and he paid dearly for whatever he did. I paid for his sins too. I gave my child away because Denton and his father and his grandfather terrorized me.

"He never liked living in this house, Father. He felt that Lafayette was too small, too constricting for him. He was a big adventurer and needed open spaces. He preferred living in Burma. He loved the people and the culture. He said that in Burma he felt free like the wind. As many times as Mother tried to talk him into moving back, he always refused. But Mother came to love Burma as well in time. They're both buried there, side by side. Don't believe what Parvati said. It was a true love story. They fell in love the moment Mother stepped off the boat. All those years, they never stopped loving each other. They were so lucky that they had each other. But now I'm old and I don't have anyone. Just these backstabbing friends, and a mean, unloving niece that I can't forgive. Who's going to remember me when I'm gone?"

"You're a survivor, Carolyn," Margo told her. It was her experience that the older people got, the harder they struggled to survive. "I have a feeling that you'll be fine. And with all his faults, remember that Claude loved you. When Father Armand asked me to come see you, he told me that he noticed the way he looked at you. His eyes always smiled. That kind of stuff can't be faked. He really loved you, Carolyn. He was weak and greedy, but at least he really loved you."

"I'll try to remember that. I'm going to miss him terribly, though. I feel like my universe fell apart when I lost him. You're supposed to get used to people dying around you as you get older, but that's not true. He was the only joy in my old age, and I don't know what I'm going to do without him." Carolyn looked sad and lost. Her eyes were red and teary, but she wasn't crying anymore at least. She was probably out of tears.

"Now Carolyn, don't forget you have a grandson. I think your daughter might be dead, but he is very much alive. I didn't have enough time to look into his private life as well. It was by pure accident that I came upon this letter."

"I don't believe you," Carolyn said and turned to Margo.

"Listen to this," Margo said taking a letter out of her pocket. "It's a letter written by your daughter.

'Dear son,

'Please promise me that you won't tell her who you are. She might reject you like she rejected me, and I don't want to see you get hurt.

Finish your studies and come back home to us. Your father and I love you very much. What do you need those rich folks for?'

"And so on and so forth. She mentions a friend, a cookout in the neighborhood, and a new dog. Then at the end she writes: 'Swear to me, son, that Carolyn will never know who you really are.' It's signed Margaret. You named her Margaret after your own mother, didn't you?"

"Dear God, yes I did." Carolyn took the letter out of Margo's hand and stared at it. "But who is it written to? Margo, please tell me, to my grandson?"

"Look at the envelope. It's addressed to Pierre."

"It's not possible. How can it be?" Carolyn was getting very agitated and stumbled to a chair and sat down. The letter was shaking in her hand as she held it. Then, they heard a deep masculine voice coming from the foyer.

"Yes, it's possible, Grandmother. I'm your grandson."

"Why didn't you tell me?"

"Because I promised my mom I wouldn't. And the time never seemed to be right."

"But I didn't treat you properly. Was I ever mean to you? I'm so sorry. You should have told me. I'm so confused." Pierre sat down next to the old woman and grabbed her hand.

"You were never mean to me, don't worry. On the contrary. You gave me time off to study, you fed me well, and you paid me extra when tuition was due. You were a good grandmother. Actually, when I first found out you existed, I came to this house looking for a job so I could get vengeance for what you did to my mother. But I couldn't be mean to you. You were too sweet."

Margo looked at those two and decided it was time to go. She put the report on the coffee table and headed for the front door. She turned around to wave goodbye, hating to intrude. But Pierre jumped up.

"Wait. How are you going back home?" he asked her with a worried look on his face.

"Benoît called me a taxi. I'm going to pick up a rental car at the airport and then drive to Half Moon Bay. Bye now. Good luck to you both. It was very nice meeting you." She turned to the door. Benoît had already opened it for her. She hated goodbyes.

"No, wait," said Pierre, hurrying after her. "Let me take you."

"Oh, don't worry. The taxi's here already."

"No, not to the airport. To Half Moon Bay."

"Goodness, no. It's too far. Then you'll have to come back by yourself. I'm used to doing this. I travel on my own all the time. When I first moved down South I drove all by myself from the other side of the country. It took me about ten days. Driving to Half Moon Bay is nothing compared to that."

"Please let me. After all you did for us, it's the least I can do. We could stop in Baton Rouge to eat something. I know a place…" And Margo remembered the smile of a young man who she had once loved dearly, and she sighed. He had also told her *I know a place* and she relented.

"All right then. Let's go." She walked over to Benoît and gave the startled little old guy with the marvelous melodious voice a big hug. "You're my hero, Benoît. I'll never forget how you captured Denton with your surujin. You know, I'm going to miss you the most. Take good care of yourself."

Pierre helped her into his car and started driving. Margo looked back at the house one last time and noticed that Benoît hadn't moved an inch. He still had that starry look in his eyes. She was really going to miss him.

Thanks for reading! Please add a short review on Amazon and let me know what you thought!

Don't miss the next Margo Fontaine Mystery:

The Black Rose Returns

Introduction

MARK DRISKOLL COULDN'T SLEEP. Something was different. Something had changed. Perhaps the waves were rougher, or the wind whistled a little louder. He turned sideways on his uncomfortable cabin bunk and tried to settle down. The air had cooled down considerably, and he reached for his quilt and pulled it over his shoulder hoping that now he would be able to drift off. But he couldn't get the images of the beheadings out of his mind. There had been so much blood. Sleep just wouldn't come. Of course it didn't help that the sloop was groaning as if it was about to fall apart.

So he gave up with frustration and got up from his bunk. The movements of the waves were getting more and more erratic. He hung on to a low beam to keep from falling, and a worried look crossed his young, handsome face. There was something wrong with the way the ship moved. Something was definitely off.

Dinner was not sloshing around in his stomach because he had already thrown that up overboard earlier, right after the massacre, but the violent movements of the ship nauseated him, and he desired to heave anyway.

THE VANISHING BLOODSTAIN

Avoiding the books falling from the shelves, and the other random objects being tossed around the cabin like nature's playthings, Mark Driskoll reached for the one remaining thing on the desk: his brown leather-bound diary. You had to be a fool not to know what was going on out there and what your odds of surviving it were. But taking things in stride, as any brave Englishman would, he grabbed his waist pouch and strapped it on. Wrapping his diary in the best oilskin he could find in a hurry, he slipped that between his chest and his shirt and hoped it would stay safe and dry. That—and the few gold pieces in his purse—would be all he needed in an emergency. Careful not to bang his head on the low beams, he opened the door of his cabin and went outside.

To say that a storm was raging would have been a waste of words. Rather, it looked like he had stepped into a madness in which the world had become a cesspool of angry gray water, and the sloop was its toy thing.

With a superhuman effort, he made it up the last few steps that separated his small cabin from the deck. The waves pounded the ship, and the winds tried to blow him back down to his cabin, but he hung on, determined to get up on deck and see for himself what was going on.

The sky was almost completely dark in spite of the time of the day. He tasted the rough salt in between his teeth as he swallowed mouthfuls of sea water. Waves swept through the slippery deck methodically, but still he held on. Staring at the thunderclouds and the lightning that spilled from them, he counted the seconds between the strikes and realized that the worst of the storm was barely a few minutes away. But truly there was nowhere to go. There was no use pretending that he could save himself. Might as well man up and meet his maker bravely, and quit shivering like a school girl.

But it was the aloneness that hit him the deepest. It grabbed at his chest, and he had to push down the sudden panic rising from it. He was all alone on the sloop. The deck was completely deserted. His first thought was that the drunken sailors, caught by surprise, had been swept overboard. Then he considered the two little boats, stolen earlier from the merchant ship and strapped precariously somewhere out back to the rigging. He figured that they could have launched those and left him to drown, if they had noticed the storm approaching with enough time.

Mark Driskoll stood in the doorway undecided, trying to think. A noise coming from the cargo hold a few feet away sounded like people screaming, and he paid attention. Then he remembered that the slaves had been locked in—and like him—they had probably been forgotten; or simply left behind to die.

There was nothing he could do about it. The wind was too strong, and he would never make it to the padlocked cargo hold without being swept away. But he reconsidered. He was as good as dead already. No harm in trying. He screamed back *I'm coming* but his words were swallowed by the wind. On all fours, and hanging on to whatever he could find, he reached the padlock, but it was tight, and it refused to open. The sheets of rain kept slapping his face, and the salt water burned in his throat and his eyes, blinding him. But he would not give up.

The slaves were desperate. He could hear their cries and their prayers above the howling wind. There were children down there too. They banged on the trap door, begging to be let out. Mark didn't even dare think of the terror they were going through in the total darkness below, feeling that the storm was raging on, but knowing that they were trapped and would be unable to get out. Eventually, the sloop would turn on its side, and it would begin to sink. The cargo hold would begin filling with water, and soon the slaves' ankles would be sloshing in it.

THE VANISHING BLOODSTAIN

Then, faster and faster, the level of the water would rise, filling the cargo hold with the freezing, cold water, and it would reach their knees and then their waists. And they would know there was no place to escape to, and they would huddle against the fear of the rising water, and they would pray, the women holding the children against their breasts. Prayers would give them a little hope, for a little while at least, because you never did lose that last glimmer of hope, and they would pray and chant their hymns and their native songs, and the water would continue rising, relentlessly. By then, only a tiny corner of the sloop would have a bubble of air left, and the strong would push the weak away to get to the barely breathable air, not caring that they were condemning them to drown.

Then, more and more of the weak, probably the women and the children, would be pushed away to certain death, and the live ones would be fewer and fewer. But eventually all the air would be gone, and there would be nowhere to go as the sloop slipped faster and faster to the bottom of the sea. Next morning, after the storm was gone, looking at the bright blue sky and the calm, gentle sea, nobody would suspect that three dozen slaves and a lonely Englishman had drowned—abandoned in fear and agony—on a broken ship. All traces of them would have vanished. Mark swallowed hard and shook the terror off. He had to try to get them out of there, no matter what.

He looked up at the sky. The worst of the storm was approaching. Now, one lightning strike followed the next with just seconds in between. Struggling pointlessly against time, he wiggled the padlock with one hand while he held on to a protruding piece of wood. It wasn't working, but—obsessed now—he couldn't let it go. He felt he ought to keep trying. He kept looking around for something to beat the padlock with and suddenly spotted a long, thin piece of metal stuck in the nets.

Agnes Makóczy

There was nothing to do but go fetch the metal bar. The wind was brutal. Fighting the waves of water and the cutting spray in his nose and his eyes, he managed to crawl to the piece of metal and retrieve it. Then, knowing how easily he would be swallowed by the sea if he didn't hold on to something, he tangled himself in the rigging so he could work with both hands.

He beat and beat the padlock, fighting the fury of the storm, slipping and falling and then slipping again. His mind already knew what his heart wouldn't accept, that the poor devils were going to go down with the broken sloop and stay at the bottom of the sea for all eternity.

He was getting dizzy with the exhaustion and the violent tossing of the sea. He couldn't continue, and he stopped. He dropped the metal bar, and it fell with a reverberating clang. His hands were bleeding, and yet he had accomplished nothing. The slaves screamed on and prayed. But he, Mark Driskoll, was done living. He looked up at the mast and the canvas torn to shreds and admired its dreary beauty against the pinkish, purplish light of the hidden moon. It was over.

Then, he saw the little monkey screeching with terror up the top of the main mast, dressed in its carnival best, somehow still wearing its little red fez hat. He'd forgotten all about little Maddock. Poor little monkey. It might survive for a while as it was tossed about the seas, as lightweight as a little monkey can be, especially if it found some flotsam to cling to. But wasn't floating for days and dying from thirst and madness a worse fate than a quick drowning?

Mark Driskoll looked up sadly into the howling darkness and thought about everything he had hoped to accomplish and now never would. At that moment, he heard the infernal crack of the breaking mast that signaled the death of the sloop and knew it was all over. It was all over for him and for little Maddock, and it was all over for every single unfortunate soul below deck. And right he was, because at that moment he saw rise from behind the sloop an impossibly enormous wave that seemed to reach as high as the sky. It came frothing furiously against him and the damaged sloop, and he barely had time to utter a quick prayer before everything went black, and he sank into oblivion.

Flash Flood Warning

MARGO FONTAINE STOPPED SINGING and turned the music off. It just dawned on her that it had been miles and miles since she had driven by the last gas station, and now she looked at the fuel gage and the blinking warning light with dismay. She was running out of gas. How could she have let this happen? She was daydreaming with Jack again, that was how. It was this lonely stretch of Louisiana highway that reminded her so much of the many times she had driven back to Half Moon Bay, hoping that she would see him again. She had allowed herself to be carried away by her memories.

But no wishful thinking would ever bring Jack back. It had been first a youthful fantasy, and then a wish almost fulfilled. But now Jack was gone forever, probably dead out there somewhere in the war-torn desert, and here she was, driving toward Pierre in hopes of turning a new leaf in her life, in search of that ever elusive happiness.

A shiver of dread ran through her body, and she turned her attention to the red warning light. She wondered what she was going to do. As far as she could remember, there hadn't been another car on this lonely stretch of road for at least a half hour.

She could always call Brooks for help, but she had no idea where she was. What would she tell him? All she could see was a narrow, endless road without a name, and very bad weather coming. Already the clouds gathering on ahead were getting darker and uglier by the minute, threatening a violent downpour, and the wind was picking up. She could feel the gusts as they hit the car. At least she knew for sure there was no hurricane coming. It looked like the usual Louisiana thunderstorm. But what if she really ran out of gas? What if the storm hit before she could get to safety? What if a flash flood came out of nowhere and swept her car away, and unable to escape, she drowned? Was death by drowning painful? Was it quick? She tightened her hands on the wheel and tried not to panic.

She was driving straight into the storm, and there was nothing she could do about it. Looking at the ugly black clouds ahead, she quickly considered her options and realized that turning back was not one of them. She didn't have enough gas for that. Besides, the road was too narrow to turn the big Mercedes around, and the ditches on the side were too deep. She would probably slip off the road and then what? Wait to die of drowning in the gutter? Her only option was to keep on going and find a safe place to stop.

Up ahead, the sun had just about vanished, filling the sky with a threatening gloom. She grabbed the wheel tighter, struggling against the wind that pushed the car sideways toward the ditch. Pouring out of the angry clouds, lightning brightened the sky and shook the car violently. She had to get off the road. But where? There was not an inhabited town, not a gas station, not a turn-off. But she had to do something. She pushed down her increasing anxiety and kept on driving.

She was in the middle of nowhere. But then, when you drive the Louisiana back roads, you often are in the middle of nowhere. All she had seen for miles and miles were abandoned farmlands that time had turned to shrub. Scattered around the landscape, you could see—here and there—a rotting barn or a horse shed, leaning away from the wind, deteriorating under the wild Louisiana weather, unfit for shelter. If there had ever been farming communities around, they were all gone now.

A big fat raindrop plopped on her windshield, and then another one. The rain had arrived. She fumbled with the unfamiliar controls trying to remember Brooks' instructions about turning the windshield wipers on. Drat. This is what happens when your chauffeur insists on driving you everywhere. She was a stranger in her own car.

At the end of yet another abandoned little town, she stopped under a decaying railway bridge and fiddled with the controls until she got the windshield wipers and the headlights working. It was amazing how dark the sky had gotten in just a few minutes. And more bad luck. The GPS was on a search-can't-locate loop and refused to work.

Should she stay under the crumbling bridge until the storm passed? It seemed more of a hazard than a safe location. But surely, if there was a railroad bridge, there was a town nearby. Wasn't that the way it worked? She kept on driving tentatively for a couple of miles, looking to her right and her left, scrutinizing the road for a road sign, a turn-off, or a mile marker. Sometimes, turn-offs meandered parallel to the railway tracks for a while and eventually led somewhere.

She was so distracted by her musings that she almost missed it. Suddenly, behind some overgrown shrub, a narrow road, its entrance almost covered by weeds appeared out of the monotonous landscape and without overthinking it, she turned the wheel.

She swerved sharply to the right. But the movement was too sudden, and the back of the big, heavy Mercedes skidded on the moist, sandy blacktop. She held the wheel tightly in her sweaty palms and rejected the urge to slam on the brakes. Her heart hammered in her chest as the car swerved first to one side and then the other. Still, she held on tight.

By now, a steady rain began drumming on the car's rooftop, and the wind whirled up twigs and dry leaves that banged on her windshield, getting entangled in the wipers. Margo's hands shook as she struggled with the skidding tires and the diminishing visibility.

Time stopped briefly as it seemed that Margo was going to careen off the road, slipping, sliding, getting ever closer to the edge. But by a last minute reprieve, she managed to straighten the car and sang out a grateful Hallelujah! She had been this close to ending up in that ditch. Now, if only her gas would last long enough to get there—somewhere—all would be well.

The back road she was following was surrounded on both sides with tall forest trees whose tops got lost in the rainy haze. Their fronds swayed and shook with the wind and threatened to snap off and throw themselves at her car. The wind howled and shrieked, and her heartbeats pounded in her brain as she held on tight. But a sudden burst of sunlight shone at the end of the road and she realized that she was almost there, wherever there was. She could already see the angry, frothy sea at the bottom of the sloping decline. She wasn't that far at all. She would be there in a few minutes. She exhaled the breath she had been holding in forever. She was going to be safe.

The momentary relief was very short, though. The brunt of the storm came down much faster than Margo expected. It went from a few steady drops to a vicious downpour in a matter of seconds, and the sun vanished completely. The windshield wipers beat the water away in a patterned staccato but they were not fast enough. Soon, she could barely see a foot ahead of her. A river of water, running down the slope with her, threatened to wash the car away. The winds kept getting stronger. They howled over the rhythmic thump-thump of the windshield wipers.

Margo slowed down to crawling mode and drove in the middle of the road with shaking hands gripping the wheel. She barely dared to breathe. She wiped one sweaty hand on her pants and then the other. Her knuckles were white, and her eyes hurt from all the squinting. The minutes seemed to last forever, and on and on she drove, focused on remaining in the middle of the road, keeping the car steady so it wouldn't get washed away.

She finally reached the end of the road at the bottom of the incline and paused at a small circular roundabout that appeared out of the pouring rain as if it had been a phantom materializing out of the fog. In front of her and in the center of the roundabout stood a nondescript stone or concrete statue barely visible in the all-encompassing rain, and beyond that—presumably—the slate gray sea.

Catching a big lungful of air, Margo rested her head gratefully on the head rest and waited for her heart to calm down. Her whole body was shaking, specially her hands. She could feel every heartbeat pounding in her temples. She was in overdrive.

To her left, an almost empty parking lot in front of a beat down hotel seemed inviting enough, and she parked as close to the front door as she could. Suddenly, she was so relieved that she had decided to leave her cats Ice and Fenway at home, even though they liked Pierre and would have enjoyed spending a few days with him in his Cypremort Point bungalow. At least they were home and safe. She picked up her cell phone and dialed.

"Lucy, it's Margo," she told her housekeeper, screaming over the roar of the storm. "I got caught in the rain and had to stop, but I'm okay."

"So where are you now?"

"I have no idea yet. I took the only turn-off I could find and now I'm in front of an old hotel in some little town by the beach. I'll stay here until the storm passes."

"Mr. Pierre just called. He was worried about you driving in the bad weather."

"Lucy, can you hear me? Oh, there you are. The reception's really bad."

"Yes. I can barely hear you. It's raining cats and dogs here as well. I said Mr. Pierre just called."

"I heard you." Margo turned the windshield wipers off. "There. That's better," she said. "Please call him and tell him I have to reschedule. Hello? Lucy?"

Margo stared at her phone in anger. She played with the buttons and she shook it, but nothing. The line had gone dead. Well, at least she had managed to tell Lucy that she was safe, and Lucy could let Pierre know as well.

She sat still for a bit and watched the rain come down. It was a wall of water. It felt like the whole world was going to wash away. She could sit in the car and wait the storm out. But as much as she dreaded getting out and facing the gale, there was no way to know how long the rain would last. She would be better off indoors where there was a chance to eat something and use the restroom. She steeled herself. Grabbing purse, keys, and phone, and with shoes in hand, she jumped out of the car and faced the storm.

The coldness of the rain and the strength of the wind caught her by surprise. The drops felt like ice needles as they lashed her body and scraped her skin. Clutching her purse and her shoes, she put her head down to better push against the wind. She was running in three, four inches of water that swirled around her ankles for a few seconds and then headed furiously downhill toward the ocean, threatening to pull her along. Pebbles dug into the soles of her naked feet, and she banged her toes on the cement curb when she reached it, but she got to the door. She was soaking wet to the bone, but she was okay.

The Drunken Duck Pub and Hotel, she read out loud through the falling curtain of water, eyeing the peeling gold colors painted on a wildly swinging sign in front of the door. It portrayed what looked like a drunken duck holding a frothy jug of beer. She pushed the heavy glass door and entered. A raft of wet wind and dry leaves spilled into the room with her and then slammed the door shut behind her.

About The Author

Agnes Makóczy spent most of her college years in Lafayette, Louisiana, attending the same school where Pierre—Margo Fontaine's Pierre—studies Engineering.

For years she gazed out of her kitchen window wondering what the big world out there was really like. One day, tired of dreaming of adventures, she packed one suitcase and left her old life behind.

An avid traveler, she now lives in Budapest, Hungary with hubby Bill and puppy Frodo until she finishes her next book. She travels as much as she can, excited to have a chance to see the world. Because life is too short, and the world too amazing, to stay in one place forever.

"The World is a book, and those who do not travel read only a page."
– Saint Augustine